RETOLD:

Heart Journeys

RETOLD: *Heart Journeys*

Faith, Courage, Stories of Biblical Women
Reimagined

Nikolai-Andre Alexander

ISBN: 978-1-0698814-0-3
Parallels & Parables Press
62 Coach Hill Dr.
Kitchener, On
www.nvsinclair.com

DEDICATION

God in Christ Jesus helped me write this book. Reading the Bible from Genesis to Revelation changed my life and my writing.

To my son, Zayn Alexander—

Because of you, I matured.

CONTENTS

Preface

For over a decade, I sat with the idea of writing a story based on characters of the Bible, set in the modern day. In 2024, I started watching Tim Ross and was led to read the entire Bible. From that, the narratives, the people, the humanity of those we tend to immortalise, came alive in my mind's eye, and I saw them as real people, with real lives and relatable issues. The idea for *Retold* was born. A year later, I had seven stories whose main characters were all women because their voices were not present in the text and I was drawn to speak on their behalf.

These stories are not sanitised because the Bible they come from isn't sanitised. My prayer is that these stories will give readers an insight into how down-to-earth and relatable the Bible is, because we have a literal down-to-earth and relatable God who works with real people with lives that often suck.

For readers from strict backgrounds who are uncomfortable with a certain level of human nature in creative work, please be advised that this book may trigger your sensibilities. Abraham and Judah, for example, are not saintly patriarchs in this book. I wrote them as they are in the Scriptures. I wrote them as imperfect men who made terrible choices.

A trigger warning for the Tamar and Gomer (Gamara) stories for references to physical abuse and adult content.

I made an extensive effort to stay true to the Text, while using contextual analysis and psychology to draw out and illustrate the emotions and subtext of the people who lived in what we now read.

Khavah

(Eve)

"It's all yours,"

Adam Mann shielded his eyes from the purple-orange sunrise that threw warm, piercing light onto the tinted glass of the agro-processing factory that rose before him and Theodore Elroy. The factory stretched thirty-six feet upwards and spanned a hundred thousand square feet. Adam stood, slack-jawed and took it all in; the rows of glass that filled the building with light, the parking spots that lined the factory in either direction, the soft ash plumes that rose from multiple smokestacks dotted across the building. He could barely make out the horizon of the roof, the size of the building causing him to crane his neck to take it all in.

Adam inhaled until he was near light-headedness and breathed out slowly. The hem of Theodore's white terry-cotton dress shirt played in the soft breeze. The older man had both hands in the pockets of his slacks. Adam loosened his necktie and breathed again. Theodore had really brought him here; he was really handing him the operation. Adam shook his head and pursed his lips to ward off the incoming tears. Theodore had been mentioning this from back in Adam's formative years, but to actually be here now made Adam's mind swim with memories and myriad thoughts.

"Let's take the tour. We'll start in the middle by the offices and work our way through." Theodore led Adam through the double-door front entrance and toward a line of office doors set in the back wall. The lounge area they walked through was an open, airy symphony of fruit, caressing Adam's nose individually and in concert. The door accommodated the salt-and-pepper-haired, broad-shouldered Theodore and the slightly taller, leaner Adam with room for two more people. Adam welcomed the significant drop in temperature and more subtle lighting that allowed him to drink in the cafe, cushioned chairs, hardwood tables, armchairs, chaise loungers and stunning wall art that accented the walls behind it all.

Searching for the origin of the aromas, Adam scanned the lounge, turning his whole body as he went. Theodore's green eyes sparkled, even as laugh lines danced across his face above his beard. Adam's similarly verdant eyes were wide, searching, hungry to devour the room.

"The smell—or should I say smells, are coming from back there. Fresh produce arrived this morning to start production."

"Are they from the farms? Yeah, no. They must be from the farms, obviously," Adam said. Theo smiled, nodding.

Noting the offices for President, Financial Officer and other company officials, Theodore directed Adam through the doors which led to the receiving dock. Sterile food grade pallets of fruit in nondescript boxes poured from a dozen tractor-trailers on forklifts and ride-on pallet jacks. Hi-vis vest wearing staff moved about at a relaxed, purposed pace emptying pallets, directing traffic, and operating machinery across the factory.

Having donned their vests earlier, Adam and Theodore stepped unto the receiving area where Theodore signalled to a young man passing with a cart of granny smith apples; the young man nodded and threw two of them in quick succession. Adam caught his as Theodore had done and bit into it, the tartness causing his face to twinge and his eyes to water.

"We'll use these for jams, jellies and other sweets. But let's finish the tour. Leave the learning for later on; we have time," Theodore said between bites.

Team leads and passing workers shook hands with them as they traversed the factory. Adam met food chemists, quality assurance specialists, order packers, forklift operators, and sanitation staff. In the few hours it took to navigate the whole building, Adam had heard possibly every version of "Welcome! Looking forward to working with you."

Everyone was cordial and that took the edge of anxiety off. His feet and ankles, however, ached by the time they were halfway through the massive building.

I should've worn more comfortable shoes. Theo has loafers on, probably with gel insoles. I did not need a suit and pointed dress shoes.

His excitement had evolved into notetaking on a tablet shortly after they left the dock area. He had started out trying to learn all the names of people but there were entirely too many. Eventually, he shifted his focus to the departments, production lines and other key aspects of the business. Six pages of notes later, his left wrist cramped from keeping the tablet in place so that he could type with his free hand. They turned left and walked down a long hallway. Adam's heels making contact with the freshly scrubbed floor made dully echoing clacks. A massive mural of trees heavy with fruit covered both walls, the rich colours under the crisp but warm lighting gave Adam a chance to breathe again. Halfway down the hall, office doors started to pop up intermittently, each one set as if under the shade of a mango, orange or pomegranate tree. Adam released his left hand from active duty and allowed it to fall to his side. His right hand slipped into his pocket, mirroring Theodore who was now whistling a tangibly familiar song. The tune filled the hall until the painted leaves seemed to undulate alongside the fruit and branches painted onto the walls. A small group of workers chatted their way into the hallway from the well-lit entrance that Adam identified as the lounge area they'd entered through. His shoulders fully relaxed as he waved to the passing crew. Smiling, they acknowledged him and the still whistling Theodore.

"So," Theodore said, tasting his mint infused chai as they sat in a pair of charcoal recliners set against another mural of abstract fruit trees flanking a magnificent ice-blue river that split into four channels, each flowing in a different direction. Around them, a steady hum of conversation had resumed after the silence that had marked their entry into the lounge. As soon as Theodore had walked up to the snack counter and started making tea, the attention of the room slowly shifted to what it had been prior.

"What do you think of Ayden Agro-processing?" Theodore continued.

"It's a lot, sir. A lot," Adam said, taking a sip of caramel mocha.

"It is, isn't it? Don't be overwhelmed though. There's time to get into the fine details and get to work. For the next few weeks though, just immerse yourself in each department and learn, observe. The only thing you need to worry about right now is naming the product lines."

"I'm naming the product lines?"

Adam paused mid-sip and hastily swallowed his drink; grateful it wasn't still piping hot. Theodore sipped his chai; laugh lines played across his forehead and the corners of his eyes. He nodded. Adam sat back in the recliner and sighed, smiling.

"You've been coming up with names and concepts since you learned to talk." Theodore said. He set his chai down on the carved wooden coffee table between them and took a bite of a confection bursting with a medley of Honeycrisp apples, grapes, kiwi and pure peach nectar.

"Fair enough. But I still don't know much about this kind of stuff outside of what you've taught me over the years. And that was out in the fields. Maybe I should get a degree, and you can keep running Ayden until I'm done."

Adam scratched at his trimmed beard and frowned. Theodore had told him Ayden would be his, but the scope of it sent pulses down his back.

A hundred people on staff, maybe more. Dozens of product lines? Yeah, I can name them but then what?

"Do I have a degree?" Theodore asked, his chai hovering at his lips. The almost-drained cup had stopped steaming. Adam set his own mug on its coaster and prepared to go make his mentor another cup.

"No, but you have six decades of experience and multiple successful businesses you've run," Adam said.

"And you have time. There's no rush. Trust me."

"That's kinda hard, sir. This is huge."

"I know, that's why I'm here. All things in their own time." Theodore finished the cup and handed it to a now standing Adam.

"Thank you, son," Theodore said. He savoured a piece of the tart while Adam worked at the coffee and tea station, refilling both their mugs.

"By the way, I want to introduce you to someone later. She's working in one of the coffee shops and I think..." Theodore's mug again hovered near his lips. Adam sat, reached for a fruit tart and looked over at the older man.

"Sir, are you trying to set me up with someone?" Adam said, still chewing. Theodore donned his usual smile.

"Yes, yes, I am. I have a feeling about her, a good feeling."

"Uh, okay. Does she even want to meet me?" Adam asked, ignoring the way his heart had started to race.

"She does."

“What did you tell her? Who is she? Where is she from?” Adam said while he subconsciously held his breath. Theodore had mentored more young adults than he could put a number to; Adam hadn’t met any of them. This mystery person would be the first.

“I’ll introduce you around next week this time. Ask her yourself when you meet her,” Theodore said. His chai was already a third finished. Adam chuckled and sat back in the recliner.

***

One year later

Khavah lounged on the wicker loveseat on the balcony overlooking the ocean of trees that flowed below. She caught up her auburn hair in a scrunchie to stop the shoulder length soft curls from blocking her line of sight. Green the colour of her beloved’s eyes was spotted with reds, oranges and yellows that, at the right angles, shimmered like a sunrise of stars against a verdant sky.

She stretched out her tanned legs and yawned. The lounger was low enough that her legs actually touched the ground. She picked them for that reason. Adam’s legs usually stretched across to rest next to hers when he sat in the other seat. He jutted out from most of their furniture like fruit weighing down a tree branch. Khavah grinned. It wasn’t her fault she was shorter than him.

Besides, the furniture needs to match.

Adam was still asleep; they had been up until late talking. They'd been up many nights—and days—talking. Adam was a tidal wave of words, feelings and emotions which had, prior to their wedding, only showed up in whispers of sea foam in their phone conversations and coffee dates. Khavah smiled, she'd prayed for a man who was open, one who shared. He listened too, which was a refreshing bonus.

He'd spent their courtship devouring her words. At first, she'd sit in the coffee shop on her break, hoping this man would hurry up and talk before her time ran out. Instead, he sat there and let her tell him everything about her day, her pastries, her customers, her marketing ideas for making the store better. The only thing he'd ever said much about was Theo. If she mentioned Theo, the strain on his face was adorable as he waited for her to finish speaking. When he'd proposed six months after their first date, she wasn't surprised, nor did she feel like she needed to say no. Maybe it was because he was her first boyfriend, maybe it was because Theo had mentored them both for their whole lives, maybe it was the fact that he fixed his eyes on her and drank her words like they were sips of spring water captured mid-flow. She'd fallen in love with him from day two. Day one had been just a tad awkward, and her heart had been too full of butterflies and anxiety to process anything else.

They had talked about fruit, and fathers, and fears and he'd told her everything he'd promised to share once they married. The way he'd opened up from the first night of the honeymoon onwards had almost made her heart explode. She was excited to delve into the business that she was now head of marketing for. She was excited to grow it into something beautiful with him. The fruit waving at her in the soft dawn breeze beckoned her to work.

"We should get ready and go in soon," Adam said from behind her. He stood stretching and yawning at the foot of the four-poster pillow-top bed that was heartbreaking to leave behind. The plush duvet and cloudy pillows made waking difficult. Adam's eyes were slightly red-rimmed, he'd told Khavah it was not a big deal but the tight shouldered stance, tense muscles and fidgety posture he assumed whenever he talked about the factory said otherwise.

"Everything is riding on my leadership; I have to get it all right."

That response spawned and had been repeated over a month of conversation about Ayden Agro-processing.

Ever since the honeymoon almost two months before, his entire mood had shifted into this rigidity that at first had fully excited her, she had been ready to get to work. But being that worked up all the time was exhausting. Instead, she'd opted to help him talk through his ideas and plans for the company. He'd gladly accepted, making full use of her listening ear and eager questions. He was still tense, but at least the talking transformed the tension into willpower and action.

"What do you mean 'we' should get ready soon, Mr. sleepy eyes? I woke up two hours ago, made breakfast, showered, ate, read a chapter and sat here waiting on you. I'm ready when you are."

Adam flushed, squinting against the morning sun to take in her forest green overalls and long-sleeved fleece shirt, and the curly ponytail caught up above her hazel eyes and slender nose.

"Oh, uh. Sorry, I had a weird dream about fruit trees protesting and telling me I couldn't pick their fruit anymore. They had their branches folded across their trunks like arms. I was there begging, and they just turned and ignored me."

Khavah bit her lower lip to prevent herself from chuckling at the clear annoyance on his face.

"It was just a dream hun, the trees won't get mad at you, I promise."

He scowled and waved her off, headed for the master bathroom.

"Thanks. I'll take your word for it," he mumbled loud enough to leave her laughing.

Less than an hour later, they exited the garage of the home that was a part of the Ayden president's package. The two story, modern farmhouse was the perfect blend of cozy and spacious. The wrap around balcony overlooked the heavily laden fruit trees from one of the many Ayden Farm sites that Theodore owned. At over sixty years old, the home was in pristine condition, having been renovated every ten years and recently furnished with the most modern, tasteful furnishings, chosen by Theodore himself in preparation for Adam taking over Ayden Agro-processing.

As they drove the eighteen minutes to the factory, Adam's shoulders wound tighter, a spring coil under pressure.

"Hun?" Khavah ventured, resting her hand on his thigh.

"Hmmm?" he muttered, his knuckles taut around the steering wheel.

"We said we'd look at best practices to improve the yield from the inbound produce, right?" She said, her words measured and sweetened with softness. His grip loosened ever so slightly, and he stopped furrowing his brows to glance at her. Expression softening, he turned back to the road.

"Yeah, we should be able to increase volume that way without necessarily needing more raw materials," he said.

"Right, so we have a plan, that's good right?" she said, smiling. His grip tightened again.

"It is, but it's not enough. I know what you're trying to do Khav, but that plan isn't enough. It's been a year, and Ayden profits aren't growing. I have nothing new to show Theodore." Adam said. His words were tree bark in summertime. Khavah breathed deeply and restored her smile.

"Okay hun, but we could still ask him for some advice; he told us to come to him whenever. You could ask when we see him for tea this Friday, you said you would've last week, and you didn't."

"Those meetings," he said quietly. He rubbed his face with his left hand and pressed his forehead with his fingertips.

"I don't even know why we have those meetings. First, he tells me that all I need to do is learn the business and oversee it the way it is. Yet he has a clause in the contract that says there's more to be done in the future. When is that? Why is there a cabinet full of documents and plans I can't touch? What are those plans? Why'd he bother including them if it's not time for them yet? And why isn't it time? Am I not good enough yet to pull them off?" He'd sped up subconsciously and only slowed down thanks to an upcoming red light.

Khavah sighed, rubbing his shoulder. He always got like this if the conversation went in a certain direction. But Theodore had asked Adam every Friday since she'd started having tea with them if they needed his help or thoughts on anything. Adam had said no every time. She'd followed his lead, biting back the instant 'yes' that yearned to erupt from her mouth. Theodore had so much experience, and he was offering. The ocean of knowledge was right there.

"My ideas aren't enough for him to trust me with those plans. Why is he asking me if I need help when he never answers anything about those plans, I don't get it, what makes them so special?" Adam continued. His frown deepened. The car accelerated again but only briefly. He glanced at her and forcefully lifted his foot from the pedal.

"Maybe you're asking the wrong questions hun," she said, keeping her voice as soft as possible. Adam groaned but smiled at her and shrugged.

***

Khavah leaned against the wall in the spacious office she shared with Adam. He was finishing an email at the custom-built adjustable desk that allowed for sitting or standing. A burgundy recliner—Khavah's favourite—sat as an accent against the cream-coloured walls and dark blue carpet. The wall to the left of the desk was a floor to ceiling bookshelf stocked with collections from Khavah, Adam, and Theodore. Between the three of them, every book on the shelf had been read. Khavah smiled, remembering the many out of print books that Theodore had flown to other continents to personally collect. Of course, he'd ended up staying in some of those countries building water supplies or starting farms for natives who had some kind of need.

Theodore arrived at three forty-five, as he always did. Adam and Khavah had wrapped up a meeting with the raw materials department heads at three thirty and were waiting in the lounge area. By the time they sat down, most of the staff had already left for the day. Khavah adjusted the black high-vis vest so that she wouldn't sit on it and smoothed her fitted khakis before settling into the sea foam green armchair facing the 'four waters' mural. Adam straightened his own khakis and sat in the matching chair to her left. As he crossed his legs, his foot gently kicked back and forth in his nude and beige loafer.

The steady hum of people flowing out of the building into the afternoon began to die down when Theodore stepped through the front entrance. The supervisors and managers were now making their way out—after weekend meetings and shutting down their departments—were elated to see him and stopped to share quick chats with him before also filing out into the parking lot. By the time Theodore made himself a chai blend and sat in the recliner across from Khavah and Adam, there was barely anyone left in the building.

"These early shutdowns on Fridays are interesting, the teams always seem like they want to keep working." Theodore said, gently blowing steam away from the rim of his cup. Khavah smiled and squeezed Adam's hand. Adam's face shifted into a thin smile that flickered before returning to a neutral state.

"Everyone's eyes are all red and people are yawning as they go through the door though." Khavah offered, looking at Adam. Adam squeezed her hand and nodded, adjusting slightly to lean back.

"Yeah, Elle from procurement showed Khav her smart watch on Tuesday or Wednesday and she is averaging twelve thousand steps by the time the shift ends." Adam said, Theo nodded, savouring his third sip of chai.

"She says she cancelled her gym membership after she started here. Leo from shipping sold his treadmill online." Khavah added.

"I'm glad they're getting more out of their jobs. And saving some money I suppose," Theodore said. He gently placed his cup on its saucer on the accent table to his right and sat back in the ash blue, high back armchair that remained unused if he was not in the building. The staff had dubbed it 'the throne' and had avoided sitting in it out of respect for the man who'd sat in most of their interviews and reassured them with jobs that they could smile about.

"So, how are you two? Anything new this week?" Khavah looked over at Adam whose body had stiffened almost imperceptibly. Rubbing his hand gently, she all but screamed at him in her mind to open his mouth. Theodore looked at him intently, waiting.

"Adam? Is there something on your mind, son?" Theodore asked. Khavah breathed deeply, expectant.

"Uh, yeah." Adam said, "We just met with Raw Materials, and we believe we can improve the efficiency of yields from inbound produce by about seven percent if we adjust a few things." Adam said, Khavah rolled her eyes, squeezed his hand and pulled away, settling deeper into her chair. Lifting her feet to the pouf that Theodore had recommended she use when her legs started to tingle, she drank macchiato from her own cup. Adam did not look at her face, instead, he stared at a point just beyond Theodore's shoulder.

"That sounds excellent, a good idea. The farmers will appreciate you making the most of their harvests. I'll pass through the factory when you've implemented it to see how it's progressing. Is there anything else?" Theodore said before reaching for his cup. Adam shook his head. Theodore turned to Khavah, the warmest smile spread on his face.

"Khavah dear, I have a story for you. But first, how are your legs?" Theodore said.

"Tingly," Khavah answered, reaching forward to rub her calves. "But not so bad. I'm here for the story though," she said. Theodore's stories were a treat akin to the butter cookie she took a bite of. When he'd visit the team at the café she'd worked at before, he'd always told her and whoever else was on break the most enthralling tales. She ate them up.

Adam didn't ask Theodore any questions the next Friday, or any the Friday after that, or the following six Fridays. Khavah gave up expecting him to ask. He grew less and less engaged with the stories their mentor was telling, often staring off into space with his mocha going cold between tightly squeezed palms. Seeing there wasn't much she could do to cheer Adam up; she opted to soak up all the stories she'd never heard before. From Theodore rescuing a dozen goats who had worn down a fence and scattered across the hills, to learning how to build his first barn himself with no labourers in little less than a year of twelve-hour days, six days a week. In all fairness, she could see Theodore building a whole barn. He was as toned as Adam was and neither of them went to the gym nor owned any lifting equipment.

Some people just have the best genes. She thought.

Khavah looked forward to those Fridays both because of time with Theodore and time with other staff who made use of the shorter shift to relax in the lounge area before going off to their weekends. It was also the only time Adam stopped working. In the first few weeks after they got married, they toured the factory and talked together, and she was in all the meetings and accompanied him everywhere. Now, he disappeared into some department or another to work on projects without telling her where he was going. She buried herself in her marketing tasks, running numbers, greenlighting ad campaigns, and doing research on competitors. He'd turn up eventually—at their shared office—tired, with grease stains on his vest or pants.

"I'm sorry Khav, I'm trying to figure out what more I can do," he'd say. She saw the sales consistently climb and profits increase as they made incremental changes. Adam waved it all off. No matter how she reassured him that the company was thriving, he didn't slow down once they got to the factory. Some days, when he brought her along, she could barely keep up with his bounding strides as her legs tingled and her smart phone warned her of elevated heart rate.

In their home, he was still the man she fell in love with; affectionate, a bit goofy, attentive, and great at listening—until he zoned out from pure fatigue and slumped into sleep on the sofa. But at work, he gently avoided her, even in her presence. Going from one meeting to another and one machine to the other, calculating volume and yield and pining over every minute detail. Eventually, she stopped trying to keep up and let him go off on his own often. She could do more at her computer than at his side. Especially when he didn't hear half of what she said.

Now nine months into the marriage, she was almost sure she'd married two minds occupying the same body. At home, Adam showered her with affections, simultaneously apologising for 'Ayden Adam' and attempting to distract her from the fact that not once did he promise to do better with her at work. His anxiety in the factory was contagious. Khavah made use of the growing tingling in her leg to let him go off without her more and more as the weeks progressed. She roamed the different departments and got quotes, stories and inspiration from the staff or sat in their office, icing her legs while reading business blogs and forums in-between her own meetings with the marketing team.

On one of her walks through the boiler rooms, she stopped to wipe her face on her sleeve and push hair from her eyes. The combination of the fleece she was used to wearing at the heavily air-conditioned coffee shop and the eight towering vats brimming with simmering fruit had led her to a wardrobe change months ago. Unfortunately, cotton wasn't faring much better in the sticky-sweet, sauna type room with air so heavy that her clothes clung to her before she could make it past the fifth vat. She rarely came this way if she could avoid it, but she'd been aimlessly wandering and talking with a group of ladies from the sorting team and had ended up standing in front of the main boiler.

"...working for Mr. Theodore from I was fresh out of high school, he's the best. Ole man knows what he's doing when it comes to some farming," said a voice Khavah recognised but could not put a face to. Wiping the back of her neck and turning in the direction of the conversation, she paused to get another set of stray hairs from dangling into her eyes.

"I was excited when they said he was opening a proper factory. I joined as a canner for him back on the farm," said another voice Khavah did not recognise.

"I know, I was sourcing preservatives after he promoted me from the field to the barn."

"Yeah, yeah, yeah. You used to wear that stupid straw hat," the second voice said with exaggerated levity.

"My hat wasn't stupid. Anyways, I'm saying. I would've stayed on the farm if I knew he was gonna let a boy run the factory," said the first voice.

"Honestly, me too. Boy wasn't even born yet when you and people like Mr. Heylel started."

"Yeah, I still don't agree with ole Theo for firing Mr. Heylel. He had the know-how. He would've run this place right."

Khavah flushed, her face redder, despite the outward heat, and slipped past the remaining vats in haste. Forcing her face into neutrality, she stopped at the water cooler just outside the boiler room exit and took many big gulps of the ice-cold water. Chilling cramps spread through her chest and down into her stomach. Smiling at passersby, she filled her cup one last time and started making her way toward the canning area. After canning was quality assurance and then packaging, then shipping.

In the shipping area, she stood at one of the open dock doors and watched a tractor trailer backing up. She shuddered, embracing the spring air and the coolness of sweat drying on her face and neck.

How many of them talk like that? Is Adam just a kid to them? I wish I hadn't heard that; I hope he never hears any of them say those things.

Going forward, Khavah stopped walking through less trafficked areas of the factory and made sure her paths always veered clear of the boiler room. She found herself drawn into the internet forums and blogs. At that point there wasn't much more data to collect on the state of the market and with her being in the office for up to eleven hours some days, she'd crafted campaigns for the next year. Pacing the room to avoid being seated for too long, she scrolled and read and scrolled until Adam eventually showed up late in the evenings.

When she shared her forum findings with him, he was mildly interested at first and then gave such empty reactions to what she shared that she stopped telling him about them unless he asked. He rarely asked. Even at home.

The forum members were friendly, informed, and kind. She had read many, many threads on all kinds of matters, particularly on one site where retired or otherwise inactive entrepreneurs were almost always online. Many of them relished the back and forth and embraced all kinds of questions, even the ones she considered the most mundane.

She had wrestled, since overhearing the two people, with asking about the issue on the forum. Hesitation stayed her fingers for days. She'd start typing a question, then stop, deleting the whole thing hastily before staring at the blank text box. She winced at the idea that she'd say something too specific or that she was being too sensitive or that a staff member might be a member of the forum and identify her or her question somehow. Maybe Adam was on the forum.

Once again, she sat at the desk in the office she was supposed to share with Adam. He was almost never there and when he was, he was pouring over documents or sitting with his shoulders bunched up, staring at the computer screens, squinting and mumbling what she was sure were obscenities.

"Hun, we're doing well, the business is in the black, all the bills are paid, profits are steady. Why are you so worked up all the time?" She'd swallowed the lump in her throat one evening at dinner when Adam had all but ignored her the whole evening, glued to data sheets on his phone while barely eating one of his favourite meals. A year into their marriage and 'home Adam' was melting away before her eyes and resembling 'Ayden Adam' far too much.

"Hmmm," he said, eyes still transfixed on the screen.

"Adam."

"Huh, oh. Khav, I need to do more. Theodore has done all this stuff, he's won awards, he's grown companies from nothing. He's expanded all of them in crazy ways. What have I done in almost two years? Keep the company in the black? That's not enough, he handed me the thing in the black. That's like sitting in a floaty and thinking you're swimming. I haven't moved; I haven't done anything!" His tone was even, and he wasn't looking at her, but his words still stung. She could not see coffee shop lunch break Adam, or even sleepy eyes Adam. Every time he said 'I', she winced slightly while trying to keep her face neutral. She had designed and executed campaigns that had sold thousands of units of product. Her name was on the ownership documents; Adam had been insistent on putting them there from their wedding day. Theodore had signed off on it.

You said we'd be partners in everything, Adam. She thought, wrangling the hurt brimming in her chest.

"Okay hun, I disagree but okay. My legs are tingling. I'm going to bed," she said quietly, leaving half her meal on the table. Adam sighed, mumbled goodnight and went back to staring at the screen. Two hours later, she heard dishes being done. When she finally fell asleep, he had still not come to bed.

A few Mondays later, at around 10am, Khavah sat reading forum threads and twirling her curls in the office. She'd recently returned from meeting with the sales department and was rubbing her calves against the massager built into the recliner in the office.

"Hey Khav," Adam said, stepping into the office with a hefty manilla folder with a tablet on top in one hand.

"The potential client is here. You still coming to the meeting?" He was ever so slightly rocking back and forth at the door, looking from her to the tablet. She smiled and rose, gently dropped her tablet onto the desk, kissed him on the cheek and took the folder from out under the tablet before stepping past him through the door.

"Let's go hun. I have my numbers memorized; would you like me to cover anything else?"

The following Friday, they sat in the lounge with Theodore. Adam's body hummed in excitement. He'd been in much better spirits since signing the deal with the new client. They had signed after only a few cursory questions and had eaten up the presentation, literally and figuratively. The CFO of the grocery company had been so enthralled with the taste and texture of one of the jams that she spilled a dollop on her white blouse. By the time Khavah finished helping her get rid of the red-orange spot with the stain remover that Ayden staff kept handy, she was eagerly reaching for the document to sign it.

The last time Adam slept so soundly was shortly after their honeymoon. Khavah had been singing praise songs all week, the tension that had permeated their home had shifted to anticipation. Adam had avoided telling Theodore anything over the phone, saying it had to be at teatime on Friday. Adam waited long enough for hugs and pleasantries to be exchanged and for Theodore to ask him how things were before he said anything. Khavah could almost see the words pressing against his throat.

"We're doing great sir; we signed a huge deal with Kodesh Grocers! I have all the numbers here; we get prime real estate in the grocery aisles and they're gonna carry us in every store in the province. That's two stores per city, over sixty stores total! They want weekly shipments, and the forecast says we'll move an additional twenty percent in volume just from them alone. And because we've got them, we should be able to reach out to their competitors as well because they didn't negotiate exclusivity. Sir, this is it!" Adam said. He teetered on the edge of his armchair like a child anticipating their favourite scene in a movie.

Theodore, smiling, sipped his chai and looked at Adam. He nodded, closed his eyes and nodded again.

"That is wonderful, Adam! Just wonderful, you are doing exceptionally. Kodesh is a well-known retailer. You can email me the documents, and I'll take a look later today," Theodore said.

Khavah shivered. Adam's face drained of colour.

"Theodore? This is a huge contract," Adam said. Every word was clipped, twigs broken in heavy wind.

"It is, Kodesh is a large retailer. I am very proud of your efforts," Theodore said, unfazed.

"That's it?" Adam said. His voice reached a volume Khavah had never heard from him.

Khavah winced, Adam rarely used that kind of tone, and usually he apologised for it immediately. Theodore was clearly pleased, proud for sure. He was smiling and nodding. That was essentially a jubilee for an eighty-year-old. She glanced at Adam sidelong, aching at the look on his face. He'd known Theodore longer than she did. This was Theodore's default demeanour. He'd been like that when she'd interviewed to manage the café in her hometown, he'd been like that at their wedding—he'd cried there though, and smiled, a lot. But he wasn't the audible cheering, animated type. Adam's expression screamed that he'd forgotten who Theodore was.

"Adam, son. You're doing well. I am proud of you. And I was proud of you before Ayden, I was proud of you when you took up the position," Theodore said.

"Khavah, how is your health? Are you still having those pains in your legs?"

Her breath caught and she glanced at Adam, who looked like a popped balloon on a stormy day. Grimacing, she turned to Theodore and forced a smile.

"I have an appointment with a specialist next month. There's pain but it's bearable if I don't sit down for too long," she said.

"I see, I pray you get good results from the doctors. Why next month? They have no availability sooner?" Theodore said, rarely seen frown lines creased his forehead momentarily. Khavah made herself avoid making eye contact with Adam. She could barely make eye contact with Theodore, who had stopped sipping his drink and was focused on her, fully.

"Unfortunately, no. Next month, the 6th, is the earliest available appointment unless someone cancels." She replied.

Is it okay to hope someone cancels their appointment? She said inwardly.

"I see. Well, all things in their own time. It'll be okay."

Theodore took a deep breath and smiled at her.

"Adam, I'm proud of you, you did well, both of you. You do well," he continued.

The tenor of the rest of teatime was subdued, with Theodore telling them—mostly Khavah, because Adam had all but completely zoned out—about experiences friends of his had with doctors and how most of them worked out exceptionally. While it did put Khavah at ease about her own medical concerns, she couldn't help glancing at Adam every so often and wishing Theodore had shown some visible excitement.

Should I say something? She thought. The weight of not looking at or reaching for Adam was crushing for the next forty minutes.

Palpable silence followed teatime. Khavah strained to sleep beside Adam that night; his phone light bled across the whole room for hours, accompanied by him turning and tossing as he read whatever was on his screen. Eventually he slammed the phone down on the nightstand and was a ball of restless fits of movement until sunrise. The next morning, they were both red eyed and weary. They were red eyed the day after that. And the next few days until he saw her yawning on the car ride home and didn't come to bed that night. In the morning, after getting slightly more sleep, she found him asleep at the desk in the home office which had previously remained unused. Khavah groaned, she'd spent half the night waiting for him to show up and the other half having stupid nightmares about the forum moderators stealing her thoughts and projecting them onto the walls of the boilers while Ayden staff snickered about Adam being 'just a kid.'

"Good morning Khav, hope you slept okay. I made breakfast," was just about all she got out of him after a while. She'd wake up and find him in the kitchen doing dishes and listening to some podcast about entrepreneurship. Words jumbled in her throat and clung to the insides of her mouth, refusing to leave. Adam indirectly cancelled the next month of teatime meetings by scheduling business calls and trips with Kodesh Grocers on Fridays. Theodore simply smiled and waved when Khavah saw him passing through the factory.

***

Adam paced the halls of the orthopedics office with a phone in each hand. He hadn't put either one of them down the entire ride over. He also hadn't said a word to Theodore who drove them to Khavah's appointment. Her knees and ankles were swollen and constantly throbbing. Their family doctor had set this appointment months earlier, after deciding that if prescription strength pain killers weren't doing anything for her, then she needed a specialist. Everything was white and smelled like cleaning supplies. Pictures and diagrams of bones, joints, and other body parts pockmarked the walls. Between them were posters of medication with names only medical professional could pronounce. Theodore hummed a soft tune while holding ice bags on Khavah's knees. With her shoulders bunched up from holding in a thousand words for Adam and Theodore and a hundred screams from the eternal thrumming in her joints, Khavah focused on breathing slowly and massaging her thighs because touching her knees or ankles caused pain to radiate into her very core and leave her nauseated.

After almost an hour of waiting—even though Theodore had gotten them there on time—her name was finally called. Adam was halfway down the hall scrunching up his face at his screens. Rolling her eyes, Khavah shuffled into the room and gratefully shimmied onto the narrow exam bed with a ream of tissue paper stretched across it. Many painful blood and fluid tests, a few x-rays, and two joint assessments later,

Khavah was diagnosed with arthritis and chronic venous insufficiency.

"You're many years too young to have these issues Mrs. Mann," the doctor said dryly. Khavah bit back a retort and a pain induced grimace and said,

"Well, I have them, so what now?" After another spiel about medical terms she had no interest in, the doctor printed out a page full of meds and treatments. Forty minutes later, Khavah limped from the building, supported by Theodore on one side and Adam on the other. His free hand was still on one of his phones, running calculations. She was pretty sure he hadn't heard a word of her diagnosis when she'd explained it to him and Theodore. The whole time they'd been in the building, he hadn't checked on her once. He was only holding her now so they could get to the car quickly.

I want my Adam back.

***

As the pain progressed past her knees and into her thighs, Khavah stopped walking the factory and simply alternated between standing and sitting at the adjustable desk. After realising the amount of side effects most of the meds would have if she took them long term, she opted to only use them when the pain was unbearable. With most of her marketing tasks and meetings taking only a few hours a day, she took to hiding among the threads on the forums.

How to grow your company on your own?

How to prove you've earned an inherited business?

Best ways to expand a business

Best ways to reduce costs

Things you need to know as an entrepreneur

Thought nuggets from her university days connected seamlessly with the ideas and insights of people on the ground. Her days were swallowed up in comment chains and conversation. She was learning but none of it was enough to show Adam. None of it would get his attention.

"Maybe you need more than just a post, maybe you need a real chat. I'd like to help." Those words played like a soft jazz instrumental on repeat as she read other posts. One of the forum moderators had posted an offer to directly answer questions for people who did not want to post publicly. All his posts and responses—and there were many—were well written, eloquent, smart, helpful.

Three weeks later, her finger hovered over the submit button for a question she had typed, deleted, retyped, edited and pined over for days.

Maybe I should just talk to Theodore.

Khavah's mind's eye filled with the image of a deflated Adam sunken into the opulent armchair with the now permanent scowl on his face. She pressed submit, then paced the room for an hour, reading posts on other forums and actively avoiding her inbox. One hour drained away into the rest of the afternoon. In the car ride home, she stared out the window, chewing her lip, clenching her fists against the urge to take her phone from her purse.

The next morning, restless from a lack of sleep that night, she hurried from the car after kissing Adam on the cheek in the parking lot and almost ran to the office. The burning in her legs didn't even set in until after she'd closed the door behind herself and sat in the recliner. Adam would be in meetings or walking the factory floor, so she locked herself in the office and paced for fifteen minutes before willing herself to glance at the tablet face down on the desk.

He's not gonna actually talk to me, he'll probably just send me a link to a paid course or something.

She had decided to be a bit specific with her question, posing it as a scenario with names and industry changed. And she'd pretended to be Adam, the one who inherited the business from her mentor. And of course, her username was something random from her childhood that couldn't easily be linked back to her.

She snatched the tablet and opened her inbox. Based on the timestamp, he'd replied almost instantly, like he seemed to do for most public posts. Her heartbeat set the tempo for her to speed-read his response.

"It seems like your mentor wants you to make your own choices. That's a good foundation. You have room to take the business in whatever direction you want. Don't worry about his approval for now. Focus on the business at hand. He'll acknowledge you when you accomplish something he can't ignore. What do you want to do next?"

The small green circle in the corner of his profile icon told her he'd probably respond right away if she followed up now. She flexed her fingers and set them on the tablet.

"I want to expand the business but I'm not sure what direction to go in, I don't want to disobey him," she typed.

"Have you asked him what his plan for the business was when he handed it over to you?" the mod replied.

Khavah hesitated, her brows furrowing. Clenching her fist, she decided she might as well follow through.

"He has some documents here that he told me to leave alone for now. I'm not sure what's in them"

"Are they about the business or something unrelated?"

"They're about the business, yeah." Khavah's chest hurt from holding her breath as she read and typed and waited. As she squinted at the three dots undulating in the corner of the screen, she forced herself to breathe before her vision started to blur.

"And he said don't read them?" the mod typed.

"Well, he said leave them alone."

"I'm not sure I'm understanding. Just to be clear. He said leave them alone, but you know where they are and have access to them?" Khavah paused, looked up at the ceiling and grit her teeth.

"Yes, I know where they are. I haven't touched them because he said not to."

"But he won't tell you what's in them, and he won't tell you what to do next?" the mod was responding so rapidly that she was typing before she even had her thoughts together.

She flushed red from holding her breath once more and from the embarrassment of the line of questioning.

Theodore really is being silly with these documents. She thought. Flinching, she checked if she'd accidentally typed his name or her thoughts. Sighing in relief, she continued,

"Yeah, no. He avoids answering those kinds of questions."

"And it's your company? So technically your files?"

Pausing again, Khavah looked up at the ceiling and pouted, her pulse drummed like theme music. She hadn't thought much about the files recently because Adam had been insistent on not going into that specific cabinet in the filing room or reading any of the files that were there. When she'd asked why, he'd simply said,

"If he wanted me to see or use those, he'd have given them to me."

She shook her head, remembering Adam's frustration in that one car ride where he'd subconsciously mentioned the files. He hadn't brought them up since then. But the forum mod was right, what was the point of those documents when Adam needed an edge and couldn't find it?

"Besides, what could be in those documents anyways? Adam has tried everything. We don't even know if there are business plans there. It's probably just notes from work Theodore has done before. How serious can it be? And why wouldn't he just give it to Adam if it would help the business?" she whispered to the empty room.

"Technically, yes. But he's still my mentor and I wanna do what he asked me. Plus, if we use them, we'll lose the company. It's in the contract we signed," she typed.

"Why would you lose the company for making it more profitable? That makes no sense. That's probably not what he meant. Sometimes you have to be bold. Maybe he's afraid you'll take charge and won't need him anymore. If those documents are so important, why is he keeping them from you? Especially if they're about YOUR company, that HE gave you. You'd think he'd want you to do the best you can. I think he's scared you'll take the ideas and run with them and be on the same level as him."

Khavah re-read the message a few times, each time nodding a bit more than before. Theodore *had* been acting strangely about the business. Why hadn't he been more excited about Adam's success, personality type or not? What about these documents made them off-limits. Shouldn't they have access to everything that could help them?

"I think you're right. Thank you." Khavah said, stepping back from the desk. Her pulse roared in her ears; her palms were sweaty. After shaking her legs, one at a time, she exhaled a pent-up breath and headed out of the office.

The filing room smelled like paper, or a library, or what Khavah imagined archive rooms in government buildings smelled like. Sniffling, she passed row after row of six foot high, silver shelves. The shelves were tagged with alphanumeric descriptors denoting what they held. She sniffled again, rubbing her nose while tracing the shelf tags with her free hand.

Someone keeps this room clean. Probably Adam, he's here a lot.

She'd been in this room before, shortly after they'd come back from their honeymoon, because Adam wanted to make sure all the shelves were properly tagged and that the contents of the open-ended binders matched their tags. While he pined over the labels and alphabetization, they'd reminisced about the cool rivers of the tucked away cove they'd stayed at for two weeks. Khavah had mostly sat at the river's edge wading her feet while Adam floated downstream then swam back up against the current a few times before coming to drag her in or splash her until she chased him off.

The files she wanted looked exactly like all the others she'd passed with one exception, the folder was a robust, sealed envelope binder instead of an open-ended holder that you could leaf through and pull files from. She found it easily. The folder was unexpectedly heavy—like that time when she lifted a box of what was supposed to be baking sheets only to find that it also had a bag of water-soaked flour at the bottom—and she almost dropped it. Catching it and tucking it under her arm, she returned to the front of the filing room and sat at the tiny desk, barely big enough to open a folder without pages falling off the sides.

The more she leafed through the documents, the further her eyes widened. They detailed the results of every year of business that Theodore had experienced. Every major sale, many minor ones, every acquisition or venture, including the ones that failed and reasons why. Every tangential business consideration that would pair well with the agro-processing business model. Every contact in every province and notes on what they were willing to offer. Every potential vendor for outsourcing aspects of the business. Plus, four different paths they could take Ayden depending on the state of the market.

In the history of the parent company, Bara Selem Industries section, there was so much information that when Khavah read through it, she started to lose track of what she'd read. The section on Ayden alone staggered her. Direct contact information for CEOs and chief buyers abounded; vendor and potential business client names swam in her vision.

Adam needs to see all this. She thought, trying to catch her breath and rest her eyes.

Glancing at her watch as she sped through the halls of the office area, it dawned on her that she'd been in the filing room for something like five hours.

Switching the files from arm to arm, then finally clutching it to her chest, she searched for Adam. She'd tried calling him, but he almost never noticed when he got calls at work. At the receiving area, she found him at a dock door, checking off inbound pallets laden with fresh fruit. The aroma cleared her nose of the smell of paper; she considered grabbing a clementine but thought better of it.

"Hun, I need to show you something. Can you give that task to someone else?" Startled, Adam looked up at her and handed the clipboard off to the person unloading the pallets and followed her as she turned and headed for the office as fast as she could go without running.

"Khavah, what's wrong, what's in the folder?"

"Just follow me please. I can't show you out here."

"Khav?" Adam's voice caught in his throat, and her name barely escaped his lips.

"It's nothing bad, it's really, really good news actually. Just hurry up." She said, her own voice hoarse. They dashed through the various departments on their way back to the offices, waving to passing staff and making their hasty strides look as casual as possible. Khavah's heartbeat drummed through her. Behind her Adam wrestled with myriad thoughts.

She said it isn't anything bad, but what is it then? She can't be pregnant. We don't gamble... anyways, she wouldn't need a folder for either of those things. Is it something about the business?

They rounded the final corner before the hall that led directly to their office and increased their speed, seeing no one in the hallway. Khavah flung open the door and headed straight for the desk. Almost dumping the contents of the folder across the desktop, she motioned for him to sit and went back to close the door.

"Read hun," she half-whispered, her voice carrying softly across the room.

"Khav, what is this?" Adam asked, failing to mask the panic in his voice.

"That folder, the one Theodore didn't want you to see yet," she said softly.

"Khavah, no. He explicitly said to leave this thing alone."

"It's too late, just open any of the files and see for yourself." Adam frowned and grimaced several times, fighting the urge to look down. Pushing away his chair from the desk, he rose and started to pace the room.

"Khav, honey, we have to put these back. He said not to read it."

"Adam, just take a look, the folder is here and what's in it will change everything. Just go look. It's fine." Frozen in place, Adam grappled with the thoughts that hit him so hard his chest started to hurt.

He said no. He also hasn't said much else other than no. He barely acknowledged the Kodesh deal. He barely acknowledges anything. I can't please him. Maybe his own stuff will please him. But he said no. It's already here though and he wrote it so it must be amazing. But he said no... We're far beyond that now. I might as well...

Ten minutes passed with Khavah leaning against the door and Adam standing in the middle of the room, rooted in his thoughts. Looking up at her, he sighed, walked towards the desk and sat. First, he reorganised the files in order of entry number, then he opened the first folder. Khavah's breaths came faster and faster as his eyes widened the way hers had. The sparkle—in those oceans of green that she'd once loved staring into—returned.

Adam's face changed from wide-eyed to slack-jawed to brows furrowed to eyes looking up at the ceiling while he calculated or tried to remember something. After a few minutes, the tingle in her legs returned and Khavah walked over and collapsed into her recliner, watching her husband devour the information like a desert in a thunderstorm. He didn't even notice her movements.

Absent-mindedly, he reached for his tablet and started to make notes, furiously tapping away at the screen while his eyes barely left whichever file was open in front of him.

"This... this is..." he whispered without looking up.

"Amazing! I know. I told you, well, I didn't say amazing at the time but yeah. What are you writing?" she asked through a huge smile.

"Oh, uh, I'm getting so many ideas. This changes everything. We have to implement these, ASAP."

Nodding, Khavah heaved herself out of the recliner and went to get her own chair. They poured over the documents that entire evening, into the night and through the morning. After showering and changing in the office bathrooms, they both napped, curled up in the moss green leather sectional in the entertainment room adjacent to the office. Waking to an alarm an hour later, they were back at it. Hunched over the files, they ran numbers and compiled digital lists of contacts.

"I can't believe we didn't think of any of this." Adam said, shaking his head while swallowing some of the coffee he'd made hastily while Khavah stretched her legs to ease the pain.

"I mean, we did think of some of these, but we didn't have the contacts to pull them off," she replied, straightening from her last round of stretches.

"We also didn't have the right approaches for most of them. I was so caught up in running the business that I didn't realise we could leverage the business itself to expand it. Embarrassing how obvious it is now that I see it in Theo's handwriting." Adam said.

"His handwriting is so neat. But I can see why he typed up most of it. There's just so much information here."

"Man, we have to implement these right away. I was so dumb not to see these. These will make the business so much better."

"I was thinking the same. The marketing stuff in here is like freshman year stuff. Some of these are actually painfully obvious; the solutions were right in front of us the whole time," she said, taking her seat and pulling her laptop closer.

"I know, right?" Adam said, "Like optimizing the boiling process so that the remaining liquid solution is cycled to other similar products. That's gonna save us gallons of water."

"Or the one about outsourcing all the packaging material from overseas, that's so dang obvious, it hurts. I'm sure that crossed my mind and I dismissed it because I was thinking that our suppliers are old partners of Theodore's."

"But he's the one who wrote it here! We should've done these things months ago!" Adam said, palming his face and shaking his head.

The next few days were a blur for Adam and Khavah, they only left the factory once to collect a few changes of clothes. Before either of them realised, it was Friday again. Looking at each other, they simultaneously shuddered.

"Teatime," Adam mouthed, no sound escaping his throat. Khavah flinched, looking down at her fingernails. They hadn't seen Theodore in weeks but now he would show up in a couple hours and be waiting in the lounge.

"Let's stay here and keep working, maybe he won't show up." Khavah offered, her words stained with doubt.

"Nah, he's coming. He loves his chai... and talking." Chuckling nervously, Adam looked back down at his screen and started clicking and typing. He swallowed against a lump in his throat and ignored the way his heart promised to thump its way out of his ribcage.

Less than an hour later, his phone rang.

"It's him," he said, fighting back the sinking in his stomach.

"Let it go to voicemail. Maybe he'll have tea by himself like he's been doing."

A gentle rap on the office door and the turning of the knob five minutes later made them both recoil in their seats.

"Oh no," Adam whispered.

"Good afternoon, Adam, Khavah. It is good to see you both. I've missed you both terribly."

"Hi, Theodore." They said in unison. Their voices sounded like scouring pads on dry pans. Clearing his throat first, Adam continued,

"So uh, we're just finishing up some work. Aren't you a bit early for teatime?"

"I was worried about you both, what is this I am hearing about sweeping changes? What is happening Adam?" Theodore's tone was gentle, but each word hammered into Adam, launching him back to childhood memories of reprimand and correction.

"I..." Adam started.

"I was at the shipping dock and saw engineers with boiler room plans that they shouldn't have. Did you pull the files I told you to leave alone?" Theodore asked. The pain in his tone made Khavah flinch.

"I... uh... Khav gave them to me."

Straightening in his chair, pulse racing in his ear, Adam grit his teeth and looked at Theodore, trembling.

"You introduced us, you told me you thought I should date. You said she was a good woman. She gave them to me, and I took them and read them." Adam blurted, words falling over each other, drunk with unease.

"Adam!" Khavah exclaimed, glaring at him, almost rising from her chair. Her fingernails dug into the sides of the office chair and tears brimmed the corners of her eyes. Adam did not break Theodore's gaze until Theodore turned to look at Khavah.

"Khavah? Why did you take those files? What have you done?" Theodore's tone was still too even, too still. She shuddered.

"Theodore, I... was online on a forum and a moderator told me to read them. He's been in business for years and he said it would help," she said.

"A forum moderator?" Theodore asked, his brows knitting.

"Yeah, on an entrepreneur's forum called Not So Solo."

"Is he a lead moderator? Is his handle something like l-e-h-e-y-l." As he spelled out the name, Khavah paled, teetering at the edge of her chair.

"Yeah, how did you know?" She said, her words, wisps of steam, broke apart in the air, barely audible. Adam's head tilted to the side, and he stared at Khavah, his face contorted into an expression she couldn't read.

"Ah, I see." Theodore said and closed the door before striding to a chair to take a seat.

"That's Lucius Heylel. He used to work for me, years ago. In any event, that's beside the point." Theodore said, crossing his legs.

"You let a stranger tell you to do the one thing I instructed against? And you, Adam, decided to listen to Khavah over me and then blame her for it?" Theodore said. Now his words had bite. Adam straightened in his chair and met his mentor's breath-stealing gaze.

"Theodore, I..." Adam said, his mouth open, waiting for words he could not produce.

"You wanted to read those documents. That was your choice. I asked you not to read them because it was too early. The business is too young; you're not experienced enough. There are suggestions there that could make the business better in one sense but would cripple relationships and hurt the local community. I'm disappointed. Truly." Theodore said. Every enunciated word and the tears brimming around his eyes made it harder for Adam to remember to breathe.

"Sir, please."

Theodore shook his head.

"I thought you understood why I was telling you to take your time and get used to the business. I built Bara Selem over decades, not two years. I was content with Ayden being steady and staying in the black; you didn't need to grow it. Why did you feel so pressed to do so?" Theodore's intonations pleaded with Adam.

"Because I wanted you to be proud!" Adam yelled. Stunned at his own volume, he slapped his hands over his mouth.

"Are you sure? Because I've told you I'm proud of you a hundred times and meant it every time. I didn't come to tea for progress reports or success stories; I came to spend time with you both."

"Theodore, I..." Adam said, tears flowing.

"I am going to have to take command of Ayden away from you," Theodore said, sitting upright and wiping his own tears.

"Wait, what? Why? Over one mistake? I can fix things. I can undo the changes. Please," Adam said, rising from his chair.

"No Adam, you're clearly not ready. You don't have a clear grasp of the consequences of your actions. The contracts we signed prohibit you from making structural changes to the business model, modifying operations in any significant way, or changing suppliers. It also has a clause prohibiting you from using any information from that folder for ten years. I'd have given it to you when I knew you were ready," Theodore said, also rising and straightening his untucked cream dress shirt.

Adam paled even further, on his forehead beads of sweat shone under the lights of the ceiling.

"Theodore please. This punishment is way too harsh. I didn't fire anyone, and I haven't even changed suppliers yet. Please, be reasonable," Adam said. Khavah clasped her hands over her mouth, trembling violently. The still stinging slap of Adam's earlier words and the heaviness of the open folders on the table left her dizzy.

"I specifically told you, do not read the files. Leave the files alone. I also told you the contract covered everything we spoke about prior to you signing it. And I watched you read it. The contract calls for your immediate removal if you breach it. You read that part out loud and whistled. You took your idea of success more seriously than the thing that would have made you successful.

All you needed to have done was maintain operations, enjoy the benefits, and learn. You can go manage one of the farms out in the countryside. I'm taking back Ayden."

An hour later, Khavah and Adam drove out of the Ayden parking lot for the last time. Khavah sat, arms folded, scowling in the passenger seat while Adam held a death grip on the steering wheel.

"Khav," he said, glancing over at her tear-streaked face.

"Should you be talking to me? Or do you have time now that you don't need to be on your phones?"

"Khav, I'm sorry."

"For throwing me under the bus or for ignoring me for months?"

Adam cringed and his shoulders fell. He opened his mouth, winced, then sat in silence for a few minutes. Tears ran freely down Khavah's face. He looked at her intermittently grimacing and shaking his head.

"I should never had said that; I panicked. That's no excuse, you were trying to help me because I was hung up on doing more. I really am sorry. You didn't deserve that," he said. Khavah wiped her tears and refolded her arms.

Adam continued, "I shouldn't have been ignoring you either. I ignored you at the doctor's and all the time at Ayden. And for what? Now it's gone. I'm sorry Khav. It's late, but I'll make it up to you."

Khavah looked at him through teary eyes.

"I want lunch time Adam back."

<u>Six months later</u>

The rays of the setting sun stretched through the laden branches of the orchard. Behind the trees, the hidden horizon was painted orange and purple and every hue in-between. Inside the house, the sounds of Adam mulling around shook Khavah from a pleasant daydream. She sat in a smooth, hand-made rocking chair gifted to them by Theodore. She'd directed the movers to place it on the veranda after they'd settled into their new—albeit much smaller—house that overlooked the fields of fruit trees where Adam now worked with a small team of arborists, general labourers and farm hands. The three-bedroom farm cottage came furnished and fully paid for. They were now about eighty miles west of Ayden Agro-processing. Her rocking chair, a cushioned ottoman for her feet, an outdoor coffee table and matching outdoor sofa filled the veranda. The orchard was huge and bountiful, with harvests taken by the truckload. Before her, the trees swayed occasionally and the crisp breeze and faint aromas of the orchestra of fruit caressed her face.

Khavah usually spent her afternoons there, waiting for Adam to come back from the fields. He returned daily with the back of his neck red and tender to the touch from bending over in the heat of the day. Even though he had a capable team, he joined in the daily nine-to-twelve-hour routines of planting, pruning, picking, packing, and lifting required to keep the orchard healthy.

The arthritis had spread to her hips and made walking or standing for more than a few minutes unbearable. Refusing to use a wheelchair to get around, she'd opted to take a part-time, remote marketing job. The burning went away for the most part if she was comfortably seated or lying down but stung terribly if she walked more than twenty feet.

Stepping through the front door, massage oil and lotion in hand, Adam yawned and cracked his neck. After his afternoon naps, Adam often massaged Khavah's burning calves and ankles. The calluses on his palms from working with various farm tools had taken weeks to heal. At first, when he'd offered to massage her, he could barely open and close his hands. Eventually, soaking them in warm water gave him some relief. Nightly, he wore hot compresses on his shoulders and lower back while she used cold ones on her knees and ankles.

"Hey Khav, did you take your meds today?" He asked through another stifled yawn.

"No sleepy eyes, I haven't. You sure you're up to rubbing my legs today? I can bear it, you know. Is everything okay?" She asked. His eyes were red, and he was squinting against the waning sunlight.

"Yeah, everything is fine. It's just that every time the trucks come to pick up the yield, I remember what he said. Speaking of which, he's coming by next week," he said.

"When? On Friday?" she asked. Adam nodded. She lifted her feet, allowing him to sit on the ottoman and placed them in his lap. He yawned again.

Hagar

Musty wool and sheep dung odours hung in the air, a permanent reminder of where she was. But the smells no longer bothered Hagar. She swept glistening, curly tresses of bronze tinted hair over her shoulder and tucked tufts behind her ears to keep them coming loose again. A hair-wash day was overdue anyways, so she didn't mind that she'd left her scrunchie in her room.

Another dawn-until-dusk workday was coming to an end. Taking the dustpan from her cart, she stooped and swept up the minute collection of dust that had accumulated since she'd cleaned the day prior.

Sarah and Abe's manor house—with its six bedrooms, four bathrooms and one of every other kind of room fathomable—was a genuine chore to keep clean. The matching fancy furniture, wall art and mirrors that were larger than a person all attracted stray wool fibres like magnets to metal. Dust magically willed itself into existence. An old couple's house had no right being this big. Neither of them used the gym. They only slept in the master bedroom. Having to clean the whole house every day was a pointless task made better only by the fact that after doing it for ten years, she knew how to manage it so that it didn't overwhelm her. Dust trapping equipment and the rhythm of the songs she sang under her breath kept her flowing through the rooms with practiced methodology.

A few hours later, as the sun bid its farewell, Hagar made her final rounds in the kitchen with the other housemaids and the pair of cooks. She walked across the open area, covered in pea gravel that stretched before the two-storey manor. She yawned and stretched as she passed strips of manicured lawn, a stone fountain and a smattering of well-maintained topiary and headed towards the staff quarters building that was a ten-minute walk away from the main house. Once in the rooms she shared with the housekeeper Olga, Hagar ignored the audible protest of her knees and ankles as she walked past the twin bed covered in her favourite blue duvet with gold triangles forming repeating patterns across it like gold dust sprinkled in the ocean. In the bathroom she stood on her tiptoes to reach the special shampoo and conditioner that she hid atop the cabinet from the equally short Olga. She rubbed her face and gently slapped her cheeks, paying no mind to the red lines scrambling around her dark brown retinas and the crows' feet forming at the corners of her eyes decades earlier than they had formed for her mother or aunts.

My hair smells like sheep; I'll sleep after it's clean. She told herself. Stifling a yawn, she stripped off the overalls and cuffed, long sleeved denim blouse and stepped into the shower. Being on shifts with the other staff worked out in some wonderful ways. She had the shared shower to herself most days after work. Olga wouldn't be back until a few hours after Hagar was deep in sleep. Two hours later, she fell into the bed—her hair caught up in a cotton towel—and was asleep before she could reach for her phone.

The following day—her day off—she relaxed in a fold-out chair at the front of the staff quarters drinking iced karkade tea, looking out at the undulating valley of emerald-like grass. The whispers of an old thought that she had long since buried beckoned to her. The distant bleats and other animal cries came to her like ocean waves, slipping in and out of her consciousness with the wind.

I miss home.

She'd moved to this country ten years prior, offered a job as a housemaid to the wife of an absurdly wealthy livestock farmer who controlled as much land as her whole village. When she'd first arrived, the endless valleys of grass covered by sheep, goats, and cattle made her head spin. Eventually, after being sequestered in the house, and learning the ways Mrs. Sarah liked things to be done, she got over the feelings of awe and started forcing herself to ignore the ever-present smell of wet wool and dusty goat hair.

With room and board covered, most of her salary went straight to her mother and father who, over the last four years, had started to buy more food than her family needed to then give it away to members of the community. Hagar was grateful. But she still hadn't gone back. The flight was twenty-two hours one way, and the cost of a single ticket could feed her mother, father, sisters and brother for a month. Besides, if she left, she likely couldn't return to the country or the farm.

Sighing, she cleared her throat and swallowed the bitterness surfacing from tears she would not shed.

"Hagar, Mrs. Sarah says please come see her in the morning before you start your shift," Olga said as she passed, heading to the washrooms in their shared quarters. She was off to take one of her three daily showers. Hagar smiled and shook her head. The poor lady was still trying to rid herself of the clinging tang of sweaty animals. She'd cut her yellow-blonde hair in four different styles in as many years trying to reduce the exposure to the smells.

"Thanks, Olga!" She said with the feigned exuberance that the Missus required when guests visited the manor. The housemaids had all perfected it to avoid their boss's ire. Sarah was a mostly quiet woman who was occasionally snippy. For the most part she ignored her staff, and they did their job in peace.

I wonder what random task she wants me to do in some secluded part of the house now.

Hagar continued to sip her drink and gaze, ignoring the odours carried on the crisp breeze that pushed her hair from her face.

Indistinct instrumental music filled Sarah's office. The salt and pepper crowned woman hummed in time to the cadence of the tune, her head nodding slightly as she did. The door had been closed but unlocked when Hagar arrived. Sarah sat in an ergonomic office chair akin to the gaming chairs Hagar saw as she scrolled past those fortunate young people who made a living as video game streamers online. Sarah's chair had a neck rest that had been adjusted to its lowest height to accommodate Sarah's stature. Her thinning, bone straight hair lay in a single ponytail across her chest, falling into her lap. The crow's feet and laugh lines on Sarah's face were less visible as she hummed. Hagar caught the briefest glimpse of her face at rest before she donned a frown, stopped humming and pursed her lips. The floral yoke dress she was wearing today featured lilies in three shades of purple. Sarah only wore dresses, and all of them had a pattern of some sort. When Olga did the household laundry each week, a queue of dresses swayed in the wind, reminiscent of a summer garden photographed or painted with care.

I guess it's easy to wear loose knee length clothing when you don't have to stretch or bend to clean your own house. Hagar's thoughts reeled out in front of her before she could reign them in. Sensing that she might start scowling, she pasted a smile on her face and waited to be acknowledged.

"Hagar, good morning, please come in and close the door. Take a seat," Sarah said flatly, her eyes did not leave the papers she was writing on. She stopped whatever music had been playing as Hagar straightened her slate grey overalls and sat in one of the four office chairs that formed a semi-circle around the massive table covered in folders, files and stacks of paper.

"I have a very special request to ask of you. Abe and I cannot have children. We have tried," Sarah continued. Hagar's eyebrow threatened to shoot up into her forehead, but she caught herself just in time for her reaction to barely show. In any event, Sarah was still looking down at her papers. Had her boss's head been raised, Hagar would have noticed the grimace through which she forced out the words and maintained the matter-of-fact tone that she always held with the staff. Had Sarah met Hagar's masked confusion, Hagar would've beheld red rimmed eyes threatening to flood Sarah's face in a fifth wave of tears. Had Sarah been willing to speak candidly, Hagar would've heard tell of sleepless nights, expensive procedures, and unrelenting desperation.

"I am telling you this because I... we would like you to be a surrogate mother for a child for Abe," Sarah said, biting off the end of each word.

"Mrs. Mamre, I don't think I understand what you are asking," Hagar managed, struggling to keep her voice even. Sighing inwardly, Sarah looked up just long enough to meet Hagar's bewildered but unshaking eyes for a moment.

"We want you to be inseminated with Abe's sperm to carry a baby for us who will become the heir to Mamre farms when Abe is too old to carry on," Sarah said in one breath. Hagar's chest hurt, as though her ribcage was trapped in a bra two sizes too small with rogue underwires. Her breaths came short, and her eyes were as wide as her face would allow. Her mind filled and went blank simultaneously.

"Ma'am..." she started. Her stomach did somersaults and bitterness gnawed at the back of her throat.

"Hagar, listen, Abe is getting older and you're one of the youngest house staff here who is healthy and clean and keeps herself to herself. If we had other options, believe me I would not have asked you." Sarah said. Her voice on the brink of cracking, she threw out the words before they could break in her throat.

"Ma'am I..."

"This farm has been in this family for 86 years. Abe would like it to stay for many generations. We've prayed for a baby and believed we would have one," Sarah spat every word, biting back the tone that hovered in the back of her throat.

"But the time has passed," she added.

"This is important and has to be done for the sake of the legacy of the farm."

They had to have an heir, whether Sarah liked this approach or not. Sarah dropped her pen, dabbed the corners of her eyes and twirled her ponytail around her finger. All the while, she did not dare raise her head to meet Hagar's horrified stare.

Hagar closed her eyes; across the canvas of her eyelids strode her family back home, grinning from ear to ear as they moved into a real house with a roof that didn't leak and had no landlord. She mentally replayed videos of her siblings using the home computer and bringing home grades she'd never seen on her own school reports. Their perfect attendance records reminded her of times when she'd sold produce in the markets while her classmates did algebra and biology. Her father's stoic but oft repeated thanks tickled her inner ear. Reels of him played in her mind's eye. He knelt, tilling his new home garden, smiling and whistling, wearing his factory clothes as gardening attire now that he'd retired.

Hagar caught herself before bursting into shrill laughter or an avalanche of tears and instead started nodding. She couldn't afford to lose this job. Too many smiles depended on it.

"Yes ma'am." Hagar said. She straightened in her chair, bit her lips and kept nodding the emotions away. Sarah's stomach lurched. She swallowed hard against frantic heartbeats.

"Good. Thank you. We'll set it up for next week. The family doctor will come by and give you supplements to take and check your cycle to inseminate you at the best time. You're free to go." Sarah said, picking up her pen and reaching for her landline. Hagar's head swam. Her heart galloped. She somehow made it back to the staff quarters, ate something that she didn't taste and went to her daily tasks.

***

Hagar had avoided going over to Raf's house when she was seventeen, even though he'd made her feel like she was dancing on clouds. The way he'd wooed her had made her spine tingle. Showing up to the market daily, buying things from her that he didn't need. He came by so often that the other women started cackling and whistling before she even knew he was around. He'd wanted to marry her.

"Can you provide for my family and me? Who will help my father before he dies in the factory?" she'd asked. Hagar's tone had bitten into Raf's confidence. He hadn't been able to respond with anything other than that he loved her. But love couldn't fix their roof or send her siblings to school or pay her mother's medical bills. He'd still pursued her. Her call log had overflowed with his number. She'd never saved his name in her phone. But she knew that number by heart. Even to this day. His number and his gap-toothed laugh looped on repeat in her mind's eye.

It was dark out before she finally looked up from dusting, sweeping and wiping. Still reeling, she went to her room and lay on the floor, curled up in the fetal position. Her skin crawled and itched but nothing was on her when she rubbed her arms and legs. Eventually, she made it to the showers, and then back to her bed. Sleep did not come.

Rafi's handsome face flickered in and out of view in her mind, replaced or overlayed by Abe's white beard, wrinkled forehead and extended bald spot. She shuddered. When Abe and Sarah had visited and offered to take her on as staff, Rafi sold some of his father's goats and bought a ring. When he showed up to her house, she wept. Her chest had burned for days afterwards. He'd followed her to the airport because her family couldn't go.

He was married now, with two of the most adorable children she'd ever seen. He and his wife worked full-time, both at the same factory she'd gotten her dad out of. Her chest burned again.

This is what I get for keeping myself to myself. She thought.

***

Hagar had changed the linens on this bed hundreds of times. Now she was lying on it, with an aloof, haggard, and disheveled OBGYN staring at her body for the third time in as many weeks. The first week had been okay, he'd only asked questions about her period cycle, family history and some other typical doctor questions that were easy to answer, albeit weird. He'd also taken blood samples, but he was gentle enough and she barely noticed.

Now she was on her back in a hospital gown barely covering anything. Her fingers twitched as she constantly reminded herself that she didn't have her phone. Usually, she wouldn't need it to scroll or call home at this hour. During the days, she only ever took it out to queue up a podcast or some music. But the moment she lay in her own bed in the staff building, she'd reach for her phone and call her parents or watch videos of gymnasts doing flips and feats that would break her body if she tried them at her age. A lifetime ago, she'd wanted to vault and handspring into twists like a ballerina temporarily escaping gravity. There still was no gym in her community. The closest one was more miles away than her parents could ever afford. After that, she'd considered ballet or contemporary dance. Those dreams did not earn money. Those dreams cost time.

Hagar felt a distant pinch that snapped her back to the previously unused room, the newly installed blackout curtains, hardwood furniture that was the reason she never refreshed the layout of the room, and the hard white light beaming down on her stomach. The doctor was doing something; she did not care for the details. More accurately, she did care but did not want to start crying again. She'd done enough of that while reading about the process online. She'd already dampened her pillow too many times reading about surrogate mothers struggling with the decision to turn their body into an incubator for someone else.

As she stared at the pattern of grape vines and clusters on the curtains to her right, she allowed the few tears that had escaped to run their course to the strange pillow now supporting her head. It was much more accommodating than her own pillow and smelled so fresh that it had made her sneeze initially. She'd never noticed that this bedroom didn't smell like sheep until she lay in this bed.

"All done young lady, I'll be back to check in with you in about two weeks. You're free to go."

Hagar sat up on the bed after the doctor had stepped back and waited until he had finished packing up his tools. She huffed a dry laugh to herself, and he disposed of his gloves and some other thing she could not make out. Her first intimate connection to a man was through a catheter attached to a syringe. She was about to carry a baby for a man she wasn't married to. A man married to her boss. An old man who hadn't known her name before three weeks ago and had probably forgotten it by now.

She hadn't told her parents about any of this. Her mother wasn't well. Her father would weep if he knew.

Months later, her belly stretched out before her, making it awkward to bend and reach and to clean in general. Her duties had been cut in half but the half that remained was still increasingly difficult for someone waddling instead of walking. The pregnancy itself was eerily okay; the only discomfort was the growing pressure on her back along with the pang of something in her chest that would not go away. The monthly checkups had been straightforward enough, and she'd gotten used to the doctor's cold gloves and colder instruments. Video calling her family while hiding her growing stomach had been annoying at first; she couldn't put the phone down and walk before the camera, she couldn't lean the phone against the lamp on her nightstand while she lay in bed. When she'd had that bout of morning sickness and couldn't work for three weeks, coming up with things to tell her mom had been mentally draining.

At least she didn't ask me about getting married for a while.

As Hagar worked in one of the expansive living areas of the manor with Olga and Sandira, the conversation again drifted to the topic of her pregnancy. The staff had taken to calling her the 'chosen vessel' or 'vessel' for short. Hagar hissed her teeth and rolled her eyes and tried, again, not to join the conversation. Sandira—who was ten years older than Hagar—had been trying to set Hagar up with her nephew who was one of the farmhands. She'd been the most audible about the whole thing over the last six months.

"If you didn't want to do it, why didn't you say no? Better yet, if you'd dated Ian like I'd told you to, they would've found some other young, pretty girl to be their 'vessel'," Sandira said, again. Hagar gritted her teeth and glared at the older woman as she fluffed up and straightened sofa cushions.

"I did not ask for this, stupid barren woman is using my body as her own. He's her husband, she should be the one carrying his child. In my country, a wife who cannot bear children is useless. A wife who cannot care for her own home is also useless. See now I'm doing the work of a wife in two ways while she does nothing except lie beside him," Hagar said. Her eyes darkened to slits momentarily before she realized that she'd spoken out loud. Groaning, she went back to vacuuming the carpet with her head down.

Olga gasped. Sandira, snickering, dropped her gaze under the scowl Hagar aimed their way. Under heavy silence, they finished cleaning and rearranging then went their separate ways for the rest of the evening.

"This is all your fault, now that this girl is pregnant, she feels she can say whatever comes to her mind. For weeks now I've been hearing of the awful things she's had to say about me."

Sarah's eyes were red with tears and fatigue. Sleep had eluded her for many days, and her tears now ran freely. Abe lay in their bed beside her, his arm covering his eyes. Sarah had been sitting up with a book in her hands. It was 4am. She had no idea what was on the last four pages of the chapter she was reading. For over a month, she'd barely left their room, trying but failing to avoid the hum of rumours of Hagar badmouthing her to the other staff.

Sarah stared at Abe and nudged him with the spine of the hardcover. He groaned and rolled over, turning his back to her.

"She's your maid, do whatever you want with her. You're the one who suggested this whole thing. She works for you," he said.

Sarah scowled at him but restrained herself from hitting him with her book. Why hadn't he said no when she suggested it. He'd just shrugged and accepted. He hadn't hugged or held her or even asked how she was doing in months. He'd seen her crying. Whenever he came in from the fields, she was holed up in the bed. Did he think she was reading for fun? All day? Every day?

"I don't even know why I bother," she said under her breath. Abe turned to look at her and squinted against the light of her table lamp.

"I don't know either," he said, turning back to his side. Sarah placed the book on the side table and slumped into her blanket. Tears formed rivulets down her drawn cheeks.

***

When shifts were posted for the upcoming fortnight, Hagar swore they were a mistake. She was scheduled for the basement cleaning—a job that had been put off from before she'd started working at Mamre because no one used the space—and her shifts were all 'continue to completion'. She'd only ever gotten 'day' shifts, sunrise to sunset shifts, or the occasional night shift if there were going to be guests the next day.

Olga and Sandira had never been in the basement in the twenty-two years they'd been there. Only a few of the men had ever been down there to store old furniture. That Sunday morning, she made her way down the creaking stairs and flicked on the yellow light, let out a guttural wail and almost collapsed on the landing. The basement stretched from one end of the manor to the other and was full of old, forgotten furniture, clothes, stacks of books and magazines and other random stuff covered in layers of dust so thick that she immediately started sneezing and had to retreat to get masks and a face shield.

Five days later, she no longer needed the mask, and the basement was no longer grey with dust. Wine red furniture that had been retired over fifteen years ago was now identifiable. Her ankles throbbed so tangibly that she almost fell over while trying to lay down a blanket on a freshly vacuumed chaise sofa so that she could sit.

At close to midnight, Hagar staggered from her bathroom into bed; she'd barely made it through showering. Her lower back and shoulders buzzed with mind-numbing stiffness. Now that she was horizontal, pain radiated in nauseating waves from her ankles. Her sides ached from the protruding belly and the constant bending and stretching from cleaning the entire basement of the manor by herself over the last week. The deep burning in her hips had remained constant and relentless. She was covered in balm and muscle relaxing creams that did nothing, and the fact that she could not take any pain meds felt like a slap. She groaned and lay on her side, stuffing the spare pillow under the crevice beneath her stomach. She hadn't been able to sleep on her stomach for over five months. Sleeping on her back felt like she was being choked and stifled, and her sides were numb from rubbing against the sheets so often.

The next morning, she was summoned to the basement and made to stand there while Sarah inspected the entire area, end to end. The old woman pulled at her ponytail while walking through, passing her fingers over surfaces.

Occasionally, she lowered her head to sniff a piece of upholstery or to inspect an area that was not well lit.

"Now that this is done, you will support the men for the next two weeks. They'll be cleaning pens this week. You're to do their laundry, clean their quarters and prepare their meals."

"Ma'am, what?" Hagar said, then immediately covered her mouth. Thoughts of her bank account stifled the swear words that effervesced from her soul.

Is she trying to kill me? Is she trying to kill her husband's baby?

"Those are your tasks, is there a problem?" Sarah said, her eyes were slits of seething ire.

"No, ma'am."

The general smell across the property was manageable. Hagar had always been able to ignore it. Up close, it nearly drove her to her knees as she did their laundry and worked in their quarters. Sun-baked milk stains, mud, dung, urine, and grass stains littered the khaki coloured, heavy, denim overalls that strained her wrists and lower back when they were wet. Pre-washing by hand took over six hours. Each of the fifteen men had three to five suits of work clothes plus their night clothes. After the pre-wash she had to put them through two wash cycles, one dryer cycle, then hanging them to dry on the clothes lines behind the quarters. She filled all five washers and still had loads left over. The whole process took more than two full twelve-hour shifts to complete.

"Aww man, I thought you'd get these stains out. How do I know my uniform is clean if it still has all the stains?" Ian said to her when he came to pick up his laundry. Hagar scowled, setting him to more raucous laughter.

"Hey goat brains, leave Vessel alone man, it's not her fault your brain is as stained as your overalls," said Oleg, a middle-aged man who was informally Sandira's partner. Hagar sighed and continued folding shirts and shorts.

This is madness. I cannot.

After soaking her feet for four hours while dozing in and out of fitful sleep, Hagar crammed her clothing into two duffle bags. She slung one over each shoulder and left the manor at midnight, picking her way along the shrubbery beside the main road to avoid being seen. Then she called a ride share and made her way into the city where she headed straight for the homeless shelter she'd heard about from Sandira. Apparently, Sarah had taken women and men from there and helped them get back on their feet. Shuddering at the memory of Sarah's burning look as she glared from Hagar's face to her stomach, Hagar settled in on the narrow cot tucked against the wall after putting down her own bed sheets. The atmosphere of infrequently washed bodies and old, over-worn, sweaty clothes was nowhere near as bad as that of sheep blood and excrement. Hagar sighed and fell asleep quickly, fatigue washing over her body.

The next morning, she skipped breakfast, instead opting to eat food she'd brought in her bag. From what she'd heard, there was barely enough food to go around, and the quality was not great. She'd overslept regardless, too worn out to rise to the call for breakfast. Eventually, she stirred after one of the subsequent checks by staff to see if she and others still in bed were alive.

As she lay staring at the wall and rubbing her belly absentmindedly, footsteps approached her followed by a shuffling as someone sat on the floor beside her. Hagar groaned and pretended not to notice.

"This is gonna sound so weird, but I'm already here so here goes," said the person. Hagar prepared herself to roll over and show him her belly and her ire if he said anything about sex or marriage.

"Return to your boss and stay there. You're gonna have a boy and he'll do great things in the future. You'll need the care that they provide. Bear the situation for now." Then the man got up and walked away. Hagar turned to her other side and stared, mouth open at his retreating form. Eventually, she lost him in the throng of muted and washed-out colours of people milling about.

"How did he know all that? What?" Hagar said quietly. "What in the world just happened? God, was that you?"

After a few minutes, she shrugged and took a nap while elevating her still aching feet on her bags. She woke up with the thought of the young man's words and sighing, took a look at her bank account. Then she lost track of time scrolling through her siblings' social media pages. Their smiles, posed in new clothes, with friends they could afford to go out with, made her stomach do backflips.

I can't really afford to go anywhere anyways.

She stayed the rest of the day to avoid the laundry that she'd likely still have to do and returned in the dead of night, slipping back in the way she had left. At daybreak, before Sarah had a chance to call for her, she showed up at her office.

I swear this lady doesn't sleep for more than four hours.

"Come in," came Sarah's voice as the music and humming behind the door stopped.

"Mrs. Mamre," Hagar said as soon as she opened the door,

"I left the property yesterday because I was overwhelmed by the amount of work you have given me. I am sorry for saying what I said about you. I was out of line. I will not say any more of those things. But that schedule was killing me. I cannot take this amount of work while pregnant ma'am. I will die."

Sarah bit her lower lip behind the curtain of hair that fell before her face as she held her head down and pretended to be reading something on her tablet. Hagar got lightheaded holding her breath in the weighted silence.

"I should fire you, since you felt the need to leave. But..." Sarah finally said, "I'll have you back on regular duties and call to have the doctor check how you're doing. When you reach the end of month eight, I'll give you reduced duty without docking your pay. Leave my office. Resume working tomorrow."

Hagar turned, stepped out and closed the door behind her. Her eyes welled up with tears that broke the boundary and spilled onto her cheeks. Behind the closed door, Sarah cursed her own womb and screamed into a pillow she had been keeping on the floor beside her desk for the last seven months.

***

On the day her baby was born—two months after she temporarily ran away—Abe showed up in the birthing room to see his son. He had opted to have a water birth on the compound with midwives, surgeons and other specialists present. Two weeks before the baby was due, an ambulance and a cargo truck drove down the winding entrance to the homestead. Out poured a dozen people with enough medical equipment to either start a clinic. The OBGYN who had inseminated Hagar, two nurses, a surgeon from the local hospital and the paramedics stayed in rooms in the manor and staff quarters. For twelve days, Hagar, Sandira and Olga catered to the people as they ate, drank, and idled.

Abe named the baby Ishmael, held him briefly, smiled, then left until he was cleaned up and allowed to be with Hagar for a moment. For the first week after Ishmael was born, Abe showed up at the same time every day to have skin-to-skin contact time as recommended by the nurses and doula who did not leave the compound. Whenever he returned the baby to Hagar, he would avoid her gaze and leave in haste. The faint lingering of his smell on the baby nauseated her and she had to ask the nurses to wipe the baby down each time. Hagar had not spoken to him before the insemination or during the pregnancy and she wasn't about to start now.

Three weeks later, Hagar swallowed the fear raking at the back of her throat and called her parents with the baby lying on her chest.

"Whose young one is that?" Her father said as soon as their images showed up on her screen. Her mother scrunched her eyebrows but said nothing. Normally, she waited to speak until Hagar's father had said his greetings, gotten a report on Hagar's health and left for his garden.

"The child is mine," Hagar said, reminding herself to maintain her native language for the call. She would have to teach Ishmael the language as well, somehow.

"We know it is not possible to return home but why did you marry without informing us? Should I not know the man who fathers my grandchildren?" her father said. Her mother's expression was unreadable. She seemed to be focusing on Ishmael's tiny little face as he rose and fell on Hagar's chest.

"Father, I did not tell you sooner out of fear and shame. The landowner told me to have his child because he..." Hagar began to explain.

"What! Is he not married? Will they also marry two wives in that country? I have not seen this on the internet. Why are you ashamed to be married to a wealthy man? You are blessed."

"Father, no. Please listen. I do not have a long time to talk with you. I am not married to the landowner. He and I did not have..." Despite herself, Hagar paused. She had rarely used that word in her language and had only used it in English when talking to Sandira. Seeing her father open his mouth, she pressed on.

"He and I did not have marital relations. They used a medical tool to make me pregnant. His wife is too old, and they needed an heir." Hagar said. She deflated and sighed at the weight that had lifted. Then her body stiffened involuntarily. Her mother was crying. Her father looked worse than he had when their old landlord had refused to fix the leaks that led to them losing the TV he had saved up to buy.

"You common whore. You... you are no daughter of mine. You disgrace your family! How will you marry? You are the mother of a bastard! You..." he said, his voice was so loud that the sound in her headphones momentarily distorted. Then he disappeared. Her mother blew her a kiss as she always did at the end of a call, and the screen went black. Hagar stared at the phone for a moment before reaching down to caress Ishmael's head. He was already a good sleeper; she would not wake him or the others in the staff quarters with the screams and swearing bubbling up in her chest. Sighing, she let the tears run and drifted off to sleep.

After feeding Ishmael each afternoon, she'd hand him over to his father and make herself scarce, whispering premeditated excuses that Abe paid no mind to. Whenever she handed the swaddled lad over, the old man's eyes immediately focused on the little head and did not lift until she returned an hour later to see to the baby's needs. The tenderness with which Abe held Ishmael left strange pangs ringing dully through Hagar's chest.

Hagar's parents no longer took her calls. After trying to call them every day for a month, she finally gave up. Her siblings texted her secretly with disappearing messages to thank her for the money that she still sent every month and for the increased amounts that came from what Sandira called the 'baby mama bonus'. Hagar had no use for most of the money anyways, she saved what she could in an account in Ishmael's name and sent home the rest. She didn't buy food, toiletries or entertainment and she had no utility bills or rent. She also couldn't leave the compound unless she did not intend to return so there was nothing to buy. Olga, Sandira and the other staff all aggressively shopped online, packages arrived so often that one of the delivery drivers was now dating one of the kitchen staff.

Hagar settled back into her own room six months after Ishmael's birth. Sarah had not been seen by most of the staff the entire time that Hagar had been sleeping in the manor with Ishmael. The moment that Hagar moved out, the Missus was seen in the halls of the house once more. Four days later, several sanitation and construction crewmen went into the manor and came out with the bed, mattress, sheets and everything else that had been in the room Hagar had used. The whole bed went into the garbage truck's hopper, the crunching sound startled Ishmael from a midday nap and set him wailing for fifteen minutes.

"The Missus has been smiling and eating more since Saturday," Olga said under her breath, glancing sidelong at Hagar who had finally gotten Ishmael to calm down by breastfeeding him with a towel over her chest. Hagar rolled her eyes and continued to gently rock him. Sandira snickered. She came within whispering distance and leaned over to Hagar.

"Your room in the manor is getting completely remodeled. They're even tearing out the floorboards and the walls of the walk-in closet. They're tearing out the bathroom," she said. Hagar squinted in the direction of the house. Her lips tightly pressed, she began to hum a song from her childhood that Ishmael had taken to.

"That's excessive," Olga said. She shook her head and escorted Hagar into the servant's quarters.

"It's getting dusty out here," Olga added.

Fourteen years later

"I shot eight ducks today mom! Eight! Without their help! Uncle Naban said the gun was a man's gun and I'm still a boy, but I proved him wrong! He was so surprised. I got the fire going and I cooked them perfectly! It was great! Dad says I'm going to be a better shot than him!" Ishmael said. Hagar nodded slowly, biting her lips and humming the first song that came to mind. His grin was as wide as the dread gnawing its way across her stomach. His hair was already growing back from the last time he'd come by the house staff quarters. He looked taller too. And there was stubble on his face. Hagar groaned internally while holding a big smile. It was a relief to see him and hug him but why did he already have stubble on his chin? His beechwood brown eyes sparkled with delight. Once again, his body was covered in small cuts and scars from trekking through all kinds of shrubbery and from climbing every tree on the compound. Well, his body was not actually little, he was already taller than her thanks to Abe's genes.

He's still a boy, why does he have to use guns so soon? She thought.

When Abe had demanded that Ishmael live in the manor when he was three, she'd acquiesced with ease. The staff quarters were cramped, and he slept like an acrobat practicing for a performance. The infrequency with which she spent time with him wore on her, but she got used to seeing him run through the hallways while she cleaned the rooms.

When she was consistently assigned to almost every room in the house except Ishamel's room, the master bedroom and Sarah's office, she'd shrugged. It was less work.

When, at five years old, Ishmael had no desire to even play with her because he wanted to walk the fields with his father, she bit her lips, cried in private and learned to deal with the outcome of her choice. She still laid eyes on him every day, prayed for him every day and stole as many hugs as she could before he scrambled out of her hands and ran off to his dad and uncle.

But hunting? The hunting made her skin crawl. Not so much the hunting as the exposure to the guns. He'd been shooting alongside his father since he was ten and she still hadn't gotten used to it. All he talked about when she did see him was types of guns, shooting competitions, and hunting. She rubbed his head, tussling the hair he'd inherited from her and hugged him fiercely, as he continued to protest.

***

Hagar woke up with a headache but paid no attention to it as usual. If it was there later in the day, she'd take a few pills and let her body flip the coin on whether they worked. She checked the fortnightly schedule on her phone instead of at the office hall. Having digital access to her shifts and pay made it easy to avoid the Missus, aside from general meetings once a quarter, and random instances in a hall here or a kitchen there, she stayed clear of Sarah's stomping grounds.

Her shifts were the same. The rooms were the same. Sarah had not repeated people shifts two weeks in a row in over sixteen years. She meticulously moved people around to keep everyone from hanging out together in the manor or pretending to clean because they'd done it the week before.

Two ambulances, a two-ton truck and three expensive cars came onto the compound that afternoon and unloaded a slew of medical equipment. The staff gathered in clusters at the staff quarters, the house, and the stables to whisper and speculate.

"Ole Abe's been up and about every day this week, he looks fit as a thoroughbred horse." One of the farm hands said in earshot of Hagar who was standing with Olga and Sandira.

"Forget ole Abe, Ishmael brought me a roasted duck yesterday, that boy can roast a duck!" said the other farmhand. Hagar smiled, despite the twinge that came from imagining Ishmael with a shotgun longer than his arm.

"Must be the Missus," Olga said, she did not whisper. The groups in earshot nodded and the murmurs grew to a hum. The equipment, nurses and doctors made their way into the manor with the help of the paramedics and the men from the truck. A few hours later, the compound settled into its regular routine, minus the cleaning staff who had all been relieved of their duties. The kitchen staff had apparently been told that the halls and bedrooms were off limits and that they were to bring food to the dining area, leave it there and exit through the kitchen only.

Speculation stayed on the lips of the staff for three days after the medical team's arrival. Hagar kept her headphones in, hidden under her hair and avoided all conversation. Ishmael hung around the house moping for the first day and a half until some of the men closest to Abe got tired of him asking and took him hunting without Abe who was also sequestered with Sarah and the healthcare people. On day three, the shockwaves of the news that Sarah was pregnant spread through the farm and lodging quarters with the haste of a hailstorm. One of the doctors trying to chat up one of the cooks, let it slip. He was escorted from the compound that same afternoon. Abe started making regular rounds in the fields two days later but said nothing to the regular staff.

Over two months later, Sarah had not been seen by a single member of staff on the farm except for the three nurses and one doctor who now permanently resided in the manor. Rumours spread about how she was paranoid she'd lose the baby, but Hagar steered clear of all conversations and went as far as to pinch her own lips between her teeth to avoid any thought from slipping into sound and being heard. Olga and Sandira teased and poked fun for days but elicited no response.

Not this time. Hagar thought. Between her own singing and the music in her ear playing low enough that she could hear if she was being called, she managed to block them out until they got bored and chatted among themselves.

In the fifth month since the arrival of the doctors, Ishmael was moved out of the house, to the staff quarters. Abe was only available to hunt once a week, and the boy ended up going with a few of the younger herdsmen more often than not. Hagar clenched her teeth and gripped her stomach every time she saw him with that rifle on his shoulder, heading out into the canopy with men much too young and inexperienced to protect her baby.

"Mom, I'll be fine. I'm really good. And I'm really careful. Relax. I'll be fin," he said when she asked him to wait until his father was available. When she mentioned Abe, he scowled, and his eyes grew wild. Her heart ached to watch him pace about the grounds with little to do when his compatriots were scheduled to work and could not go hunting with him.

The return of ambulances and more doctors three months later triggered another round of gossip. This time, news was readily available the next day, from Abe himself. All the staff were called to gather in the open lot before the manor. Abe stood before them with a megaphone and waited until the crowd was big enough. Ishmael pretended not to listen to his father, but his body language made Hagar chuckle. Then she remembered her own father and bit her lips to redirect her thoughts and stave off the tears that seemed to have been waiting at the rims of her eyes.

"Sarah and I now have a son. His name is Isaac," Abe said. As he spoke, he was smiling so hard that his wrinkles jostled for room on his face. Those closest to Abe cheered exuberantly. Meanwhile, the majority of the staff clapped as expected, but murmured out the corners of their mouths while he continued to speak.

"He already has a son though," one man a few feet from Hagar said. He glanced at Ishmael and folded his arms. He was one of the fellows who accompanied Ishmael on his forays into the outcropping of trees on the edges of the Mamre property. Hagar smiled in his direction, and he nodded in acknowledgement.

"I really wonder what they had to do to get that old lady pregnant. Good Lord." Olga said out of the side of her mouth. Sandira giggled and nudged Hagar who bit her lips so tightly that they almost started bleeding.

After the short address, Abe and his regular cronies found Ishmael, and they went hunting. Ishmael was almost vibrating with excitement as he ran to his room to get his gear. Hagar rolled her eyes at Abe who was actively avoiding looking in her direction. On her way back to her own room with Olga, Ishmael zipped past her weighed down in hunting gear but smiling like a hyena.

"Well, at least that's back to normal." Sandira said quietly. Her room was next to Ishmael's. He played his video games so loudly that it was hard for her to nap before she had her afternoon shifts serving meals in the manor.

For the next six months, Abe was markedly absent at the same two or three times every day where he usually would've been in the fields or out hunting. As a result, his timetable—and that of the timetables for everyone he was close to, including Ishmael—changed to accommodate the times he disappeared into the house. No one saw the baby himself until he was around six months old, at which point, he was only seen as a bundle swaddled in blankets or an outline in a stroller when Abe took him for a walk. Sarah still did not leave the house, prompting a round of rumours that the pregnancy had almost killed her and that she was on bedrest. Hagar rolled her eyes and promptly avoided all the unsubstantiated trash that floated around when people gathered to talk.

***

Two years later, they held a proper birthday party for baby Isaac. On his first birthday, only ten people—not including Ishmael—had been invited. The party happened behind the manor, where the high walls prevented visibility. Ishmael sulked the whole time. His video game enemies felt the brunt of his ire. Hagar went for her shift shortly after 7 am and returned just after sunset and peeked into his room. He was exactly where she'd left him, same clothes, the two-litre bottle of pop at his side was drained and the room reeked of sweat and sticky sweetness.

At this second birthday party however, everyone was invited. No one was scheduled to work. The spot at the front of the manor was brightly decorated and a dozen long picnic tables were spread out with all sorts of confections and drinks.

Little Isaac ran around chatting gibberish at the top of his voice. He was a bright red blur of joy, shakily bolting from one group of people to the next having robust conversations that only he understood. Most of the staff smiled and responded as they would any toddler and he was on his way. Having a little one on the compound for the first time in a very long time left everyone in good spirits, especially because they'd finally gotten to meet him.

Isaac eventually made his way over to where Ishmael and his friends were seated. The boy peered into Ishmael's face, standing on his tiptoes.

"What's wrong? I look like dad?" Ishmael asked. Hagar stiffened. She was standing a few feet away and like most of the people close enough to see, was drawn to this introductory interaction. Isaac continued staring and Ishmael began to frown. Then he scrunched up his face, stuck out his tongue and got up close to Isaac who screamed and ran to his mother. Sarah turned red when she saw her baby fleeing from Ishmael's direction. Hagar paled and was very glad she was already seated.

"Here we go," Hagar said under her breath.

Sarah scooped up the still sobbing Isaac, spun on her heels and stormed straight up to Abe. The only sounds to be heard for the next five minutes was the children's music being played and Isaac's slowly subsiding wails. His head lay on his mom's shoulder while he gripped her blouse as though he thought he'd fall.

The throng of staff, Mamre family members, and guests pretended to still be otherwise engaged, all while glancing at Ishmael—who was now stiff as a column beside a trembling Hagar—and Sarah who was animatedly whispering to Abe.

"Mom, dad looks mad, am I in trouble?" Ishamel whispered. Hagar groaned. The pit of her stomach roiled.

Abe frowned, shook his head and walked off after a few moments. Hagar grimaced as he walked towards her, motioned for her and Ishmael to come to him and then turned and headed towards the staff quarters. Her chest tightened with the air she held there for far too long.

Once away from the crowd, Abe sighed heavily and turned to Hagar.

"Sarah wants the two of you gone by tomorrow. I will transfer some money to your account to help you out. Pack your belongings tonight and I'll call you a taxi to take you to the city." Abe said. His throat quivered and his eyes were wet with unshed tears.

"Excuse me, what?" Because he made a face at the baby? Is the baby made of glass? Making a blasted face will kill him?" Hagar's voice carried across the yard, making her pause, but she furrowed her brows, hands on her hips and continued.

"This woman, your wife, stole my body, my chance at marriage, my whole life!" She said, her volume still rising. Abe paled and stepped back, hanging his head.

"Now she wants us to leave. And go where? Is Ishmael not your son? Are you not a man?" Abe rubbed his face, shook his head and turned to leave. Ishmael walked after his father only to hear a stern "No son. Stay with your mother. You cannot go back inside."

Hagar's brain went dead quiet for a moment, and she stood there with Ishmael beside her, staring at the ground, silent. Flashbacks of that phone call with her parents hit her in the stomach and chest. She pursed her lips, took the deepest breath she could and exhaled slowly.

"It'll be okay, Ishmael. It'll be okay." Hagar said. Ishmael threw his hands in the air and stalked off to his room. The video game was going at full volume by the time she reached the door.

That blasted woman. Why did she ask for you to be born? She's never wanted you. Did Abe even want you

Tamar

Tamar had out-sung her competition. Rawness with a tang of blood soured her mouth. Her throat burned. Her shoulders ached from being bunched up for the six days since the start of the initial auditions. She was slumped in a long, deep-seated, dark mauve couch that all but swallowed her, as her throbbing ankles rested on a matching ottoman. The waiting area of the studio felt like half of a rich person's house had been transplanted there. Tucked into one corner were the stocked double door refrigerator and full bar replete with alcohol from across the world. Against the wall where Tamar now sat were the sofa she and a few others were lazing in, two burnt gold loveseats, a double recliner and twelve paintings of different sizes that were a stunning collection from an artist who might not have been sober when they did their work.

Tamar was no longer sweating from the hours of singing and performing for the panel of judges but her layered black and bleached bob-cut hair still clung to her cheeks. She fooled around with the scrunchie in her handbag, waiting to be finished with the studio so that she could snatch the dang hair out of her face.

Gotta stop at the pharmacy and get some pain pills. She thought as she winced from the throbbing in her lower back. The red and black asymmetrical dress and stockings were getting uncomfortable now. She took solace in the cotton pajamas and hair bonnet waiting for her at home.

It had been almost two hours since she'd been informally told that she'd won and to wait for Judah Jacobs to formally address her. Twenty handpicked female vocalists had auditioned for a chance to write and record a duet with one of his star artistes, Ernie Isaacson, on his upcoming album. She'd shown up in full makeup, dresses and heels for six intense days of runs and riffs, song after song after song. She had sung from the depths of her diaphragm to be chosen above all the other talented, gifted, well-trained women. The small crowd cheering on the singers included her mom who was a retired music teacher and her best friend Raya who was a home health nurse.

One of the other competitors was in her forties and had the voice control of a well tuned piano. Trembling at the memory of that lady holding a note so long that the judge had to tell her to stop, Tamar shifted her weight from one thigh to the other and watched as Judah and Ernie took pictures with a horde of fans. Ernie's arm slipped around almost every woman who tucked in for a selfie or group picture. His butter-coloured jacket, ankle length turquoise pants and gold brogue shoes were tiring to look at. Tamar opted to close her eyes for a bit. Even some of the women who'd auditioned were among the throngs clamouring for a photo op. Her mom and Raya had already congratulated her and left for the evening after realising she'd be stuck there for a while. Twenty-five minutes later, Ernie and Judah walked over to her, Tamar quickly stood, straightened her dress and smoothed her hair.

"Tamar! You did well, and you'll look great beside my guy on all the cover art! Congrats! Let's go to dinner!"

Judah had one of those voices where you knew he could sing. He'd made album after album of great music over the decades. The way his—and Ernie's—eyes danced up and down her body made her skin crawl. Forcing a smile, she locked arms with him and let him lead the way as he talked her ear off.

Shower and PJs will have to wait. Good thing I only wore three-inch heels today.

***

"You really can sing Tay! And you can write too. We can start on the other two verses and the bridge next session; I've got an appointment. Let's pick this back up tomorrow." Ernie said, flashing her the smile he'd no doubt used to woo hundreds of fangirls. He'd been flashing her that smile for weeks. His teeth were too white, paid for white. His smile read as serpentine. Again, Tamar resisted the urge to roll her eyes all the way back into her skull and returned a smile that barely curled her lips. He blew a kiss in her direction and stepped out of the sound booth, dapped up the producer and left the studio. The whole time, his gaze never left his phone.

The weeks since they'd started working together—two months after the final audition—had all been like this. They'd spent the first session listening to instrumentals while Ernie hummed and sang into his phone for his social media fans. By the time they'd chosen an instrumental, perfected their harmonies and finished the first verse, over a month had passed. Each session was an hour or two of studio time, where they got one or two lines down on paper, then sang them repeatedly until Ernie was satisfied with the entire sound. Every syllable, every note, every run and riff, every key, every bit of harmony between their voices and the voices of the three ladies who sang back-up.

Can we just finish the song? Or at least get somewhere with it? Tamar thought. She slumped into the taupe couch behind the producer's station that faced the booth. Tamar had been recording songs since she was seven, she'd asked for studio time as a birthday gift so often that her family eventually pooled money and built her a sound-proof booth in her bedroom in her parents' home. But this studio, one of twelve in the massive Judah Records building, was by itself, half the size of her parents' four-bedroom bungalow. Five monitors and an eighty-four-track mixer sat before Jim, the short, toned sound engineer whose golf cap hid a spreading bald spot in the middle of his head. Tamar rolled her eyes and looked sidelong at a mental image of Ernie.

Jim has to boot all this up and those three ladies get dolled up and stand in heels, just for you to sing two lines, stare at your phone as soon as you stop singing and then leave at the drop of a dime. Ridiculous.

Tamar had worn heels and a dress for the first two recordings; the social media manager had taken pics of the process and Tamar had gotten some great pics out of it. Her posts had gone viral, boosting her social media presence significantly. The third week, Tamar wore lower heels and had a pair of burnt orange strappy sandals in her bag. With two sessions scheduled per week, her ankles started protesting the repeated instances of unusual footwear. Before the third week ended, she was in a nice, comfortable pants suit—with pockets—and low-profile sandals that were super easy on her feet.

Ernie didn't handle his own social media, so the notifications had to be from text messages. When his phone vibrated, he'd smirk or grin, often licking and biting his lips, clearly feeling himself. Tamar would hide her chuckle and the hint of jealousy by hiding behind her own tablet where she wrote notes and waited on him to finish so that they could write lyrics.

Half of the time though, his face progressively soured and his attention to the task at hand waned. Ernie would stand in place, before the microphone, with one finger up to signal for Jim to wait while he read and swore under his breath. In the first week, Tamar gave up her idea of the behaviour she'd come to expect from Christian men in this particular studio. The disparity between how they acted inside the studio and how they were before the media and fans gave Tamar whiplash.

On a few occasions, Ernie would get a text message, read it, and immediately storm out without a word to anyone. Tamar was resigned to go home early and practice on her own.

The engineers would roll their eyes and immediately pivot to working on a project in need of mastering or mixing.

"Girl, I'm telling you, I don't know what's going on with him, it's like his mind is somewhere else completely," Tamar said to Raya as they drank smoothies at a hole in the wall cafe near to the studio one evening after rehearsal. Raya was in sandals and a beige sundress, beside her, a large bag with her work gear sat. Tamar knew that her friend's scrubs were likely on a hanger in her car.

"Must be nice, to have enough passive income to where you can show up to work and do next to nothing," Raya said, rolling her eyes.

Tamar did see his natural talent though, and work ethic. For the hour or two that he stayed in the studio, he was focused on the task at hand. Even if he was a bit too flirty for her liking. The pace was mind numbingly slow for her though. She'd written and recorded at least one song per week every week since she was fourteen. Those songs were mostly mediocre—especially the first few dozen of them—but it didn't take a month to write and record one good song.

Two days later, Tamar sprang up into a sitting position when her phone rang and the caller ID read 'Judah Studios'.

"Good afternoon, Tamar. Mr. Isaacson has engagements that will run through next week. You will have no sessions until the following week." Said the voice of the front desk associate.

"Thank you for the update, Mrs. N," Tamar said through clenched teeth. She threw the phone down on the bed and screamed into her pillow.

At least we kinda got somewhere with the mini sessions. Now we're skipping three? At this rate, I'll have grey hair before we finish the second verse. Tamar thought. Ernie had given her his number. She'd dialed it and stared at it on her screen dozens of times. But she could never bring herself to calling him to tell him that he sucked and that he should get his act together.

Judah would blow a fuse or something. But good grief, this is ridiculous.

A few moments later, she heaved herself out of the bed, pulled her work blouse over her head and left the house.

At the grocery store she'd been at for the last seven years; she went to the shift roster and put her name down for two shifts she had not taken since she'd started recording with Ernie. Weaving around customers and other staff, she pushed her cart full of miss-shelved items, putting cans, bottles, boxes and sachets back to stock in their rightful places. As she went, she alternated between vocal exercises and random worship songs that came to mind.

"You have a lovely voice young lady. Do you sing at church?" said an older woman in a dress that screamed 'church mother'. Tamar smiled broadly and nodded.

"Yes ma'am, I certainly do."

The woman's face filled with a huge smile that added a dozen lines to her freckled face.

"That's beautiful dear. I didn't want to disturb you in your work but I'm just too glad to see someone your age singing good songs so well," the lady said as she grabbed beans from the shelf and shuffled away.

Am I singing too loudly? How on earth did she hear me? Tamar looked around, nervous that her team lead would show up and threaten to write her up. After a few minutes, her shoulders loosened, and she started humming without realising it. It was nice when the compliment about her voice wasn't accompanied by a lewd comment or an effort to get her number. Apparently, the XL blouse, loose pants, and messy bun weren't enough to ward off the attempts at least once a week by random shoppers.

Two weeks later, Tamar was back in the studio. The soundproofing sponge at her back was like laying down while standing. The engineers and technicians were busy spinning tracks into masterpieces. Ernie was late. She'd already alternated between sitting on the couch, to walking around after she nearly dozed off on the shoulder of one of the back-up singers to now leaning on the padding inside the booth. The repetition of the song that Jim was working on became background music to Tamar's rising agitation. A few times in the last three hours, she'd zoned in for long enough to listen to and memorize the whole instrumental, and the placement of the chorus, bridge, and verses. It was a catchy song by an artist Tamar was sure she knew but couldn't put a name to. Jim was busy squinting and straining to hear things that only producers hear. She still remembered that time when one of the ladies—flirting with Ernie—had leaned on the mixing board and moved a few knobs. Jim had screamed at the young lady, bringing her to tears. Usually, he said next to nothing. Tamar had shuddered and shrunk back for that entire session and was glad when Ernie was eventually dragged away by his phone.

Mostly, she stared at the barely started lyrics on her tablet, fighting the urge to write five different versions of the track.

Annoying contract. But whatever. Where is he though? My shoulders hurt. She thought as she hopped between social media apps and her personal catalogue of songs. She had at least six verses that could comfortably fit the song her and Ernie were supposed to be writing.

She was dozed off in the production room couch when Mrs. N called her cell, jolting her back to consciousness. Jim was still squinting at waveforms on his screens and nudging his cursor to make adjustments only he could hear.

"Tamar, hello dear. Please see Mr. Jacobs in his office. He is waiting for you." Tamar's heart immediately went into overdrive, and her breaths came shorter and shorter as she whipped her purse up after stuffing her tablet into it. She stood up, rubbed the sleep from her face while slinging her bag over her shoulder. Her pants were all bunched up in the wrong places, warily eyeing Jim as she tugged at them unceremoniously, she eventually felt comfortable enough and started for the door.

"Oh, Jim? I think the section before the bridge would transition more smoothly if you added the modified chorus between the verse and the bridge. Obviously, you know this, but I think the chorus creates a better crescendo before hitting you with the powerful vocals. Bye!"

She gently closed the door before waiting for Jim, who was now staring at no one, to answer.

Tamar speed walked as inconspicuously as she could down the carpeted hallway lined with awards and portraits. Thanks to the air conditioning, she didn't break into a sweat as she whizzed past door after door, her mind going faster than her legs were. The tightening in her throat led to her stomach forming a dozen knots at the thought of not being able to respond to whatever Judah had to say to her. Finally, she paused at his door and clenched her fists, squeezing until her mind cleared enough for her to catch her breath and make her face neutral.

His office door was ajar and what sounded like swearing was trickling out. She knocked and entered, stopping cold in the doorway at the sight of Judah Jacobs. His dress shirt was half untucked, his tie nowhere to be seen, his eyes were red rimmed and wild looking, his full beard looked ragged, nothing like the day of the competition when she'd last seen him. He was pacing behind his desk, beet red and with fists clenched.

"Hi Tamar, please have a seat." He said, his tone and the expression melting from his face didn't match. Beads of sweat forced their way through Tamar's makeup and slid down her face. Without taking her eyes off him, she sat in the chair furthest from his desk with her purse on her lap. Judah's expression was still steely as she sat down in an armchair that was both firm and pillow soft all at once. She squeezed her fingers together in her palms to stop herself wiping her face aggressively and prayed that a stray droplet of sweat wouldn't work its way toward either of her eyes.

Please don't ask me to close the door, please. She thought; her legs were straining to resist the urge to start shaking. Instead, she continued to wring her hands in her lap.

"I'll get straight to the point. They locked Er up. He's probably going to prison. I can't bring him back." He stopped pacing briefly and looked in her direction, his eyes softening just long enough for her to catch her breath.

"You'll be working with Onan, our next rising star. He's got that thing! Boy could sing a fish out of water. You can head home. It'll be a while before I finalise paperwork and wrap up all the court stuff."

Tamar nodded and rose from her seat.

"You'll like Onan, he's closer to your age and a great talent."

Unmistakable fondness peeked through Judah's pained tone. Tamar turned and smiled in his direction, her eyes looking his way but not seeing him. Her brain was still reeling;

the tension he was holding, though not directed at her, made her queasy.

Or I could just record a solo, she thought as she sustained the forced smile and held the doorknob like a lifeline.

"I'm sorry to hear about Ernie, that's awful news."

Her thoughts and pulse were so loud that all she could do was pray she was saying the right words.

"Thank you, Judah, for setting me up with another talented artiste, I look forward to meeting him."

***

"I heard he was an undercover drug dealer."

"I heard he beat someone up who owed him money."

"All the other people don't know what they're talking about. He for sure killed someone."

Tamar still visited the studio once a week to make use of her access card and to try and figure out what Ernie had gotten himself into. Rumours filled the studios more than instruments and vocals. Each one made Tamar shake her head or roll her eyes.

There's no way he killed someone, he had a thriving career, who throws that away? Tamar mused as she restocked shelves and hummed one of Ernie's songs under her breath. She'd been hesitant to let her voice out in the store since the old church mother had complemented her.

I don't think I sing good enough to where they won't fire me.

A bit over a month later, Tamar sat drinking a berry bonanza smoothie with Raya on her day off thinking about the artists that Judah was so proud of. It turned out that Er had racked up a significant amount of debt from buying certain classes of prescription drugs trying to 'give himself an edge.' He'd illegally acquired memory enhancing drugs that they gave to Alzheimer's patients, ones for muscle building, and a cocktail of other things that from all accounts, should've killed him. Then to pay off his debts, he'd started distributing the drugs on his tours. Prior to his arrest, at almost every session, he routinely popped different pills into his mouth. At first, she'd thought they were some kind of candy but the golden yellow medicine bottles she saw him slip out of his pockets were a dead giveaway. Now he was going to serve a life sentence for a list of crimes that made her head spin.

Raya finished her drink, hugged Tamar and headed to her SUV. She had a home visit in the next twenty minutes. As she drained the remnants of her purple smoothie, Tamar scrolled through the pictures she'd taken with Ernie after the singing competition and during rehearsals.

If you could call them that. He's a great singer, but man, he barely sang anything with me. Tamar gasped, scrolled quickly to older photos of Ernie and stared, slack-jawed at what she was seeing. Both his selfies and professionally taken photos showed him with a full head of curly sand brown hair, a full beard and a strong but soft jawline. In the more recent pictures, his cheeks were more sunken, the area around his eyes were darker, the lustre in his smile had faded and his whole body looked rigid.

He used to be prolific, putting out a song every month, featuring on every album, doing pro-bono shows all over the city, at any little church. Tamar shook her head, tossed the smoothie container into the bin and left the cafe. After pulling her sunglasses from atop her head and using them to shield her eyes from the brilliant summer glare reflecting off every surface, she took out her phone and looked at a few more of Ernie's pictures.

Something must've happened that caused him to start taking those drugs, maybe he couldn't sustain his old pace. But like, dude, you've been in the industry for over a decade, slowing down wouldn't have killed you. Your fans were loyal, and your songs were classics. Such a waste. Now I have to deal with Onan. Tamar shuddered and repressed the involuntary gag that formed in her throat.

Onan was buttery voiced arrogance in a fitted suit. He had the strong lean physique of a track and field athlete and the height of an average college basketball player. He talked slow and deliberate; every word laced with honey. Half the time, Tamar was sure people agreed to his voice before they even registered his actual words.

Yeah, he's handsome. But his ego could cause a solar eclipse.

Onan started every conversation with a grin and a wink. Especially his conversations with Tamar. She had rehearsal in thirty minutes and had chosen the cafe near to the studio for that reason. A few months ago, she'd have shown up early to just hang out but now that she was dealing went Onan, she went at the exact start time and left immediately after the end of the session.

"Tamar! Don't you look stunning today as usual," Onan said when she entered the studio. His eyes roamed her body from the silver anklet her mom had bought for her eighteenth birthday up her fitted taupe capri pants and peplum V-neck vermillion blouse. Tamar ground her teeth and glared at him before forcing herself to smile.

"Your beauty is wasted on this studio; we should go get lunch or something. The mics will be here when we get back. What do you say?" he asked, oil dripping from his words. Tamar groaned as silently as she could manage, smiled away the eye roll she felt coming on, and shook her head gently. In the studio were her, Onan, Jim the engineer and his assistant, Martin. The trio of ladies who had sung backup with Ernie had moved to another project and would only show up to add final harmonies once most of the track was laid.

"No thank you, I'd really love to work on a song or at least practice our harmonies."

Onan's smile didn't waver one bit. Nodding, he got off the counter stool he was perched on and set down his drink.

His wine-red button-down shirt stretched taut around his chest as he sauntered over to the microphone. After counting them off with his fingers, Onan raised a note from their harmony lines. Tamar blinked twice, then caught herself before he could start smirking. She listened for another few seconds and then added her voice to his, modulating as she went to match him exactly where she knew it would sound best.

The sound of his voice soaked into her as they sang, she'd never heard it in person and the way it blended with her voice caught her off guard. This was their third session, and he had spent the first two doing all manner of other things that had nothing to do with writing a new song. His voice was simultaneously refreshing and chilling, like a crisp glass of lemonade sat in a freezer for just long enough that ice had begun to form.

After they sang the first few lines, Tamar closed her eyes and let the harmony whisk her away. They ran through the practice song twice and Tamar waited; eyes still closed for him to start them off again. No melody graced her ears. Onan was already halfway to his drink by the time she opened her eyes. Her body stiffened and words she generally tried not to use bubbled up in the back of her throat. Sighing, she released her shoulders and drummed up the smallest smile.

"Taking a break already?" she asked, swallowing the intonation she was sure would get her kicked out of the studio. Through the viewing pane, she glimpsed Jim and Martin stretching and heading for the door to exit the studio. Frowning, she refocused on Onan.

"Where are Jim and Martin going? Are we finished?"

"Nah, we don't need them just to practice harmonies. They're not recording anything, and the track is still playing. We can sing whenever," he said, his voice as cool as the air that filled the sound booth. Nodding, Tamar turned to take a seat on the other side of the studio, across from the mics.

"Why don't you come sit beside me and let me pour you a drink?"

"No thank you, I don't drink alcohol." Tamar said, breathing slowly to keep her tone even.

"Oh, you don't drink? You're a real church girl then, huh?"

His unwavering smile was like a grater, her patience fell away in thin flakes.

"I'd just like to sing, if that's alright. If you want to take a break, that's okay. We can start again when you're ready," she said through clenched teeth.

"I bet you're still a virgin too then, I don't see a ring on your finger."

Tamar's eyebrows shot up, then dropped as she squinted at his statement. Catching herself, she relaxed her expression and forced another smile. In one fluid motion, her phone was out and recording audio in her hand without her looking down. Onan sipped his drink nonchalantly.

"Please let me know when you'd like to start practicing again," she said, her tone flat, she dropped the smile and kept squinting.

"You know we can practice whenever you want, we could be doing something much more fun right now," Onan said without lowering his glass.

"I bet you're the kind of girl who sits quietly on Sunday mornings and takes notes during the message. Anyways, my drink is finished. Catch you next week. If you wear something that sits on your hips so well next time, I won't be able to concentrate at all."

Tamar fought the instinct to cover her body with her hands and instead focused on where he stood in relation to her. Onan set his glass down, corked the bottle he'd been pouring from and strolled out of the room without looking back.

Who even has a bar in their studios anyways. Why isn't more singing going on? This place is a mad house. Tamar rolled her eyes, saved the voice recording and waited two minutes before leaving the studio. As she walked, she rubbed her hand over the textured surface of her phone to self-soothe and repeatedly reminded herself to breathe deeply. Onan's languid gait had made it difficult for her to storm out of the building like she'd intended to do. Slowing her pace further, she stepped lightly, so that her shoes wouldn't make any noise on the laminate floors of the lobby area. Onan was about fifteen feet in front of her, talking loudly on his phone.

"Yeah man, Judah wants me to finish this song with the girl... she's hot and everything but she's kinda stuck up... anyways, he wants me to finish that guy's song. I don't think so man. If I can get it in with the girl, great. But I sing my songs for me. I'm not having some idiot's name on my work... Who? Him? Yeah... The fool went and got himself locked up and I'm supposed to carry on for him? Forget it... Yeah... Exactly... of course it is! Anyways, I'm out. I'll catch you later," Onan said.

The halls of the studio were mostly empty of traffic; everyone was either recording or gone home. Onan was so busy scrolling while chatting into his earbuds that she probably could've crept up to him and knocked him over the head with her purse.

I'd need to jump though. And my contract with Judah doesn't cover hitting d-bags.

Tamar had waited until he exited the building and made it into the parking lot before she went out.

Get it in with who? What does he think this is? That's definitely not happening. Nasty ole...

Onan slid into a matte black luxury vehicle and sped off, giving Tamar room to breathe. Climbing up into the wine-red pickup truck she'd saved for by taking extra shifts, she sat and breathed with her eyes closed until her heart was no longer hammering. Seeing the cloud cover and swaying trees, she set her GPS for the long way home to let the breeze air out her thoughts. She shuddered as she left the parking lot. The slimy feel of Onan's stare still lingered.

"I'll have to watch myself around him," she said to the empty passenger seat. "What do I even do if he doesn't plan to write or sing anything? I can't report him to Judah. Onan will just deny it. Ugh! Why couldn't I have gotten a decent man who just loves making music and isn't a weirdo?" Gripping the steering wheel until her knuckles went white, Tamar turned up the volume on the music playing until she couldn't hear herself think anymore. Then she began screaming the songs one after another for the forty-minute trip until she left the main road and turned into her community. The old folks in her community probably wouldn't mind some gospel music but not at ear splitting volume. Tamar slowed, bellowed out the lyrics of one final song and turned into the community, ignoring the tears staining her makeup.

Tamar's heart knocked hard against her chest for the entire next session with Onan. Even in a loose fitting, puke green blouse that revealed nothing but her arms and a pair of pants so straight, they were almost a perfect rectangle, Onan still ogled her while they practiced lines. He had shown up and glanced at the lyrics they were supposed to be working on. After spending most of the session idling with the engineering team, he sang for ten minutes with Tamar, made one remark that made her want to hit him over the head with one of the mics and then left at the same time he had the week prior.

"I hope you're not on drugs too. Although maybe the third time is the charm... No, I won't wish that on you." She mumbled as she left the building twenty minutes after he had. Jim was working on a nice song that was now stuck in her head, and she opted to hang around and listen to it rather than give Onan more access to her in the open parking lot.

"It's easy to be nonchalant when your career is set in stone." She said as the fresh air whipped at her messy bun and tried to snatch her scrunchie. Tamar only showed up because she needed the song credit to kick start her own musical path. Onan could wait this out; she didn't have that luxury.

Three more sessions went by with barely any progress, Onan conceded half of a verse that took hours to write and then chose to practice it to death to avoid having to write anymore. His attempts to get her to go out with him were consistent and persistent. That annoyed Tamar more than the lack of progress on the song. After each studio session, a hot shower was the only way to remove the stain of the way he looked at her.

The engineers were nowhere to be seen when Tamar arrived for the next studio session. Onan was wearing an oriental pattern silk shirt with the top buttons undone and a smirk that made Tamar shudder.

"Where's everyone?" she asked after scanning the engineering room, couches, and booth and seeing only Onan. Offering pleasantries usually led to him starting nauseating conversations. She'd stopped saying good afternoon from the third session.

"Oh, I gave them the day off. It's just me and you today sweetie. What does a guy have to do to get a hug?" he said, advancing with arms wide as soon as she entered the booth. Tamar took two quick steps backward and reached into her pocket for her phone. She'd made a habit of being ready to record him at a moment's notice.

Onan kept advancing, his smile as oily as his shirt was shiny.

"I'm not comfortable hugging you," she responded, shoulders clenched, eyes slitted.

"Dang girl, that hurt my feelings. I promise you'll like the hug once you're resting against my chest. I'm real warm. Come on."

He was fast approaching, arms still splayed, a glint of thirst in his eyes.

"Onan, no. I'm not interested. I just want to sing," she said, she slipped her phone from her pocket, took another step back and quickly peered down to make sure that it was actually recording audio.

"I wanna make you sing girl. Stop playing hard to get. We both know I want you. You keep showing up even though we haven't done a thing to that song. You want me too; you're just dragging it out. Just let me hold you for a bit. I'll be gentle."

Tamar blinked and he was on her. Arms closed around her before she could duck out of the way or retreat further. One of those arms slid down the small of her back and fingers clasped her bottom a moment later. Tamar screamed. She shoved and screamed and hammered her fist against muscle that would not budge. He pressed her face into his chest.

"I'm recording this and it's going straight to my friend. If you don't..." she yelled through the side of her mouth. He was three feet away again before she knew what was happening. Shaking, she caught herself and stepped back quickly, reaching for the door.

"Come on girl, I was just playing. Delete the recording. Delete it!" The change in tone made her shiver. His voice was devoid of all smoothness and was now a dry, menacing baritone. But she was out of the room, running down the hallway, and calling the police before he had time to say another word. He was likely still shouting when she got to her truck and locked herself inside. Breathlessly, she recounted what had happened to her to the assault victim hotline. Sliding down below the windows, into the crevice below the steering wheel, she waited for police sirens to signal safety.

"Ma'am the perpetrator seems to have left the property, but rest assured, we will locate him," the officer said once they found her vehicle and checked the building for Onan.

"Okay, I have audio proof of what he did. Do you need my phone?"

"No ma'am, you can email that to us," the officer smiled softly, waited for a moment until Tamar stopped shaking and turned to leave. Nodding, Tamar sat staring at a spot on her windscreen until her breathing normalised and she remembered that she was supposed to have worked a shift right after the recording session. If she went now, she'd be late but could still work. As she drove, music blaring at full volume, she ignored all the calls from Mrs. N and Judah that repeatedly interrupted her playlist. It was all she could do to see through the tears as she made her way across the city to her workplace. The smell of his cologne and the alcohol on his breath clung to her nostrils. The places he'd held her felt indented, like maybe a hot shower wouldn't be enough this time.

Her shifts at work for the next two weeks passed in a fog. Tamar was on autopilot at work and at home. She stocked shelves, drove home, tried to scrub Onan's touch off her arms in the shower, failed, wept and slept. Halfway through the second week, there was a call to say that they'd picked up Onan and her recordings were more than enough to take the case to trial. The news channels and social media had already released multiple stories about him and some even mentioned Er as well. Statements like 'his career is over,' and 'there's no recovering from this' floated around in every video or broadcast. After a few days, she stopped picking up her phone to browse social media. Every time she saw his picture or heard a song, her skin crawled and she shivered. She still hadn't answered Judah's calls. She hadn't read the email from Mrs. N either. Eventually, Raya answered Mrs. N and told her that Tamar was in no condition to field calls and would need some time to process what happened.

"Girl, I'm telling you, Judah will have to withdraw whatever contract they have with him to protect the company. If they associate with him at all, it'll look like they agree," Raya said as they sat sipping iced coffee before Tamar's next shift.

She'd been the one feeding Tamar all the information about the case since Tamar started avoiding the internet. Tamar's body involuntarily broke out into shivers, leaving her covered in goosebumps. It was all she could do to not think about that night. His body had felt like iron against hers. The way he'd towered over her, cornering her.

Maybe he wouldn't have gone further than a hug.

But he didn't even get consent for the hug in the first place.

Maybe I should've dressed more modestly.

Did I overreact and mess up his career for no reason?

Her mind raced the circuit of thoughts with no finish line, no answer. Since the incident, the slightest touch from males passing by on the street or in the store made her whole body go rigid and her hairs stand on end. The cascade of thoughts made sleep elusive and fitful and left her on edge the whole time. Finally, Raya convinced her to accept the help from the sexual assault response team. After four online sessions with a therapist they recommended, she had the basic tools to self-regulate enough to make her way out of the brain fog and back to the present.

"You'll need to get the studio to pay for more therapy sessions girl, you shouldn't pay for them yourself," Raya said as she finished her coffee and prepared to go off to work.

"That sounds like a fun conversation." Tamar replied. Raya shrugged, hugged Tamar and turned to leave.

"It won't be pleasant, but they owe you."

"Hello Tamar. Please come and see me at the studio when you have time." Judah said in the voicemail Tamar was finally listening to. She'd allowed another few weeks to pass before listening to the voicemail that had sat on her phone for over a month.

I really hope he'll see the stupidity of this whole thing and just let me write and record a solo song. She thought as she climbed into her truck and turned the radio on. She didn't have a shift for work scheduled until later that night and she did want to get back to singing in the booth and possibly get financial coverage for more therapy sessions.

Her drive to the studio called for all the breathing techniques and self-talk she could remember from therapy. Flashbacks of Onan's body pressing against hers kept making her twitch and lose focus as she sped down the highway.

Mrs. N looked at Tamar askance, rolled her eyes and looked away so quickly that Tamar considered that she might've misread what she just saw. She rang Judah's office and simply said, "She's here," then waved in the general direction of the office. Shrugging, Tamar said thank you and kept walking down the hallway.

"How could you? Do you know how hard that kid worked to get here? How much I spent on his career? What is it about you that attracts problems for my lead singers?" Judah said as soon as she stepped through the door to his office

"Excuse me?"

"Onan had to be let go to preserve the label. No one will ever let him sing at this level ever again. His career is dead." Judah said, his voice was dry and sharp.

"I..." Tamar attempted, Judah cut her off.

"All he did was try to hug you. Why were you even recording with your phone? He was just flirting, you're single, he's single. Isn't that what you young people call 'shooting your shot'? All you had to do was say no and leave it there. Now he's ruined. Dammit." Judah was beet red, he was pacing through the office faster than when Er had been arrested.

"I'm sorry but..."

"Here's what I need you to do, go home. Sit out a year or two until things die down. The label took a big hit with all this bad press," he said, his tone ashen. Tamar opened her mouth to reply, but he held up a palm and shook his head,

"I have another up and coming lead you can duet with. This next artist is too young. Right now, Sheldon isn't ready to sing with anyone. He needs some more time to mature in his craft and find his voice."

Judah waved her off and turned to face the floor-to-ceiling glass wall that overlooked the city lake and surrounding trees. Tamar pressed her lips together, turned on her heels and stormed out. As she passed the front desk, it sounded like Mrs. N let out a 'hmph', but Tamar was too busy fighting back tears to care.

"I attract problems for his lead singers?" she said to herself as soon as she was clear of the exit doors.

"ME? I'm not the one drinking a handful of pills or lunging at women who clearly aren't interested. How is this my fault? Wait TWO YEARS? Is he insane? These stupid men mess up and somehow, it's my fault?"

The scream she couldn't let out burned the back of her throat. She made it to her truck and put her music to max volume before screaming until her lungs ached and her shoulders heaved. She beat the steering wheel with open palms and clenched fists until the truck shook, and her wrists throbbed.

"Stupid. Stupid. STUPID. This whole thing has been absolutely ridiculous!" Tears streamed down her face; a dozen thoughts raced through her mind at the same time. She could set the building on fire. She could blow them up on social media. She should've recorded that conversation with Judah just now. She should sue them. She should go back in and tell him to jump off a cliff. Tamar screamed again and shook her head. The tears were still flowing. She screamed again until she started coughing. A group of people were exiting the studio and heading into the parking lot by the time she opened her eyes and stopped screaming. Groaning, she started the ignition and sped out of the parking lot, peeling past them with her head straight, refusing to even see who they were.

"What in the world does he mean?" Raya said. Her eyes were wide; her nostrils were flared. She was glaring so hard that

Tamar would've flinched if they hadn't known each other since high school. Tamar shrugged and sipped her drink through gritted teeth.

"Girl, listen, I don't know how you walked out of there without telling him to... Oooh I hate that man," Raya added, releasing her grip on the table. She looked like she was about to start stuff. Tamar half-smiled and swallowed some of the creamy smoothie.

"I'm too cute for jail. I still wanna slap him though."

***

Tamar sang and practiced and sang some more. Daily home recordings quickly filled up her hard drive. Weekly therapy sessions kept her from sending a hundred feisty emails and from sharing a thousand sarcastic posts on social media. Raya had snatched her phone and sent Judah an email demanding money to pay for therapy and he'd sent the cheque to the therapist's office two days later, with no argument.

A few months after the incident, she had to testify against Onan in court while he and Judah glared at her. Then came the questions online and in-person about when she was putting out the song with the label.

Why is everyone asking me? Go ask Judah why I need a man to write and release one single song.

After the reporters and social media hounds got bored and moved on, she was hit with another problem. She couldn't sign with another label or write and release original music for three years based on the contract she had with Judah's label. She was stuck. With nothing else to do, she poured out song after song after song in her home studio and performed at every church service, concert and graduation that she could get into. Thankfully, she'd already released music before Judah Records that was outside the purview of the stupid agreement.

"Sue his butt and break the ridiculous contract," her mom said one evening at dinner as she scooped sweet corn onto her plate. Tamar stabbed a chicken thigh from the baking tray that sat at the center of the table and groaned.

"With what money mom? Judah has lawyers on retainer that destroy cover artists and DJs for fun. No thanks. I've been to court enough," Tamar said, helping herself to a large spoon of seasoned rice. Her mom shook her head, shrugged, then sighed.

"There's a lot to be said about rich old fogies in positions of power. But that would ruin our appetites. Pass the gravy please."

***

Tamar waded through the two years as quietly as she could muster. According to her contract, she technically had access to the Judah Records building until the song was published and subsequent touring ended but she had no desire to have to walk past Mrs. N, let alone see Judah before she absolutely needed to. Two months into the third year, she started checking her phone every few minutes for calls, emails, or texts that didn't come. The label didn't reach out a single time. Her emails to Judah remained unread. Mrs. N fielded none of her calls. She was pretty sure the old woman had blocked her number.

"Girl, listen, you gotta go down there. Confront old Judah and ask him what the deal is. This kid you're supposed to work with has done an EP and a full album and he's a good singer. What's the deal with them and this one song? It's one song!" Raya said, eyes bright and full.

Tamar scrunched up her face and held her tongue. After a month of Raya repeating reason after reason after reason, Tamar finally threw up both hands and acquiesced.

"Fine, I'll go. I'll go," Tamar said. Raya grinned and pumped her fist.

"I'd come with you but I gotta go keep old people healthy. Love you though. Go get your song girl. You worked for that thing!"

For days, she went back and forth before her mirror, contemplating, rehearsing, second-guessing. She knew what she needed to say to him. But she also knew how he'd react. But she was in the right, and he wouldn't care. She'd waited for the one song for years. But she'd signed a contract. To avoid freaking out her mom, she grabbed a stuffed animal from one of the chairs in her room and screamed into it.

"Maybe I shouldn't have entered this God forsaken competition in the first place. I should've known better."

Tamar suppressed a shudder as she walked through the studio. In her mind's eye, she watched herself run down that same hallway to escape Onan. With deep breaths and her fingers rubbing against her phone case, she put one foot before the other and made her way. Her access fob had worked just fine and there were so many people coming and going that no one really looked her way. Between the large, oval yellow sunglasses, broad rimmed, tweed sun hat, sweeping floral sundress, blonde wig and overly confident gait, Tamar barely recognised herself as she swept through the lobby and down the hall. A few well-placed calls by Raya had confirmed that Judah would be in the building working on instrumentals and final edits for an album that was launching soon.

Why am I even wearing this get up? She thought. With her chin high and her back straight, she kept going. The closer she got to the engineers' rooms, the more her emotions roiled. Her heart drummed up a rhythm in time with her heels on the floor. The back of her throat tingled with all the things she ought to say to Judah. A chill down her spine reminded her of Onan running his hands down her back.

Then she reached the Judah's office. The glare of his open laptop screen illuminated the awards that sat shelved behind the desk. She hesitated, peered down the hall, then tentatively called his name to see if he was in the office out of sight. She slipped into the silence that answered her and swept across the office to the desk as quietly as the heels would carry her. The laptop was unlocked. A folder full of instrumentals and unfinished songs sat there. Beckoning. Tamar's heart thrummed in time to short breaths and quick glances at the door. Tamar emailed two of the unfinished songs and the accompanying instrumentals to herself, while straining her ears to catch any sound of Judah or anyone else approaching the office. As soon as her phone dinged in her purse, she deleted the sent email and sat in the office waiting for Judah to show up. A half hour later, he arrived, smiling and humming a tune.

"Oh," Judah said, his eyes never meeting hers. "I wasn't expecting anyone today. But as you're here, how may I assist you?"

His eyes devoured her from head-to-toe multiple times as he spoke. Ignoring the thirst in his gaze, Tamar allowed the gentlest of smiles and slowly uncrossed and crossed her legs, allowing the flow of the dress to pull his eyes.

"I'm just a huge fan of your work. Your songs are amazing, and I love the work you've done with the people on the record." Tamar said. She lowered the timbre of her voice just enough so that she sounded different. Judah's chest puffed out. Leaning against the desk, he continued to drink in her body with his eyes.

"I'm sorry for intruding like this but I really wanted to meet you in person."

"That's quite alright. I'd love to take you to dinner some time. How does that sound?"

"That sounds delightful. An evening out with a man of your stature would surely be eventful," she said slowly. Every word dripped with softness and invitation. Judah licked his lips and nodded without shifting his gaze even for a moment. Unhurriedly, Tamar rose from the armchair, allowing the dress to work on Judah's imagination. She walked towards him and reached out her hand for him to take. He kissed it and rose from the desk, looming over her like a hungry wolf. Tamar smirked, dipping her chin a bit in a show of bashfulness.

Dropping her voice to a whisper, she asked, "I'd love a photo with you. I promise I won't share it on social media. But I really want to capture this moment forever."

Judah immediately straightened, ran his hands through his obviously dyed hair, tugged his shirt straight and beckoned for her to go ahead. Leaning against his chest, Tamar snapped three pictures from different angles and then turned to face him once more.

"Here, I'll put my number in your phone," she said, extending her open palm. Judah handed the phone to her, allowing his grasp to linger so that their fingers touched and maintained contact for a moment. Tamar typed in a number and handed it back.

"I look forward to your call. I won't take up much more of your time. I know you're a busy man," she said. Judah started shaking his head before catching himself.

"Yes, very well. I'll call you and we can arrange a date. It was very lovely to meet you... Ashley." He said, looking down at the contact information. Tamar made sure her stride exiting the office was slow and measured. She could feel his eyes follow her out. Holding it together until she made it to her truck, she released a huge sigh and sped off.

Oh man, that was scary. I'm never doing that again! What was I even thinking? She thought as she drove. The email notification icon on her phone beckoned to her as she drove. Three different times she caught herself speeding and had to focus on keeping to the speed limit as she neared her house.

***

"Where are my files? There are some missing from my laptop." Judah said to Kira his assistant the next morning as they went over the songs he'd been working on in his personal time.

"You mean the new songs you told me about?" she asked, opening folder after folder

"Are you sure you saved them and everything? This is why Jim recommended you work on them here instead of at the home studio by yourself."

"I still know how to record and mix a track. I know I saved them; they were here yesterday. In that folder. I went to talk to the boys in the studio then came back and that gorgeous young woman, Ashley, was in my office. Speaking of which, I need to give her a call and take her to dinner."

"Did she mess with your laptop by chance?" Kira said, eyebrows raised.

"I'm not sure, now that you mention it, but why would she steal my songs? They aren't finished, what would she do with them?"

"Well maybe not then. Regardless, you'll find out if you call her."

The number Tamar gave Judah went to voicemail after three rings. He tried a few times over the next few days and, both embarrassed and annoyed, decided it must have been a prank or something similar and deleted the number.

***

Tamar reveled in the melody of the next three months. In her quaint home studio, she recorded verses, harmonies, and ad libs to the two unreleased songs she'd taken from Judah's laptop. At first his vocals caught her off guard, even though she grew up listening to his music, the maturity and care with which he sang made Onan's raw talent pale in comparison. Judah's lyrical style matched hers so well that she spent hours swooning over them before she actually started thinking about her own additions and vocal stylings.

She took her time, writing and rewriting each line until she felt like the two songs were lyrically perfect. Then she recorded, listened on repeat, re-recorded and mixed her additions until she tingled with excitement every time she listened to both tracks. When Tamar's mother heard the songs, she ended up getting the choruses stuck in her head for two days.

"I still can't believe that's what you did! This isn't what I meant by get your song. But I'm here for it!" Raya said as Tamar recalled what happened and played the unmastered audio of one of the two songs.

"He was never gonna listen to me." Tamar said, smiling at the instrumental and vocals she'd now heard hundreds of times.

"Fair point, this song is good girl! I can't wait to hear it when an engineer works their magic," Raya said, bobbing her head.

"I know right," I should send it to Jim."

Raya snorted a laugh then covered her mouth as she continued to giggle.

"Judah would have a coronary. Maybe I should pass through for medical support." Raya said, smirking.

"Nah" they said in unison.

***

"She sent you what?" Judah's eyes bulged and the veins on his forehead peeked out. He'd been at his desk milling through more paperwork than he had any interest in when Jim called him to let him know what had landed in his email.

"Two completed songs that sound like hits. I wanna go ahead and work on them but I wanted to ask you where she found a duet partner. I've never heard this singer before." Jim said. He was talking fast, his pitch higher than usual. Judah's eyes widened even more. He slammed the desk and stood so fast that his chair rattled and his coffee almost spilled over his tablet and paperwork.

"She broke the contract! This girl just keeps hammering away at our reputation. She's got no regard for principles or ethics. Tell Nancy to get her on the phone and get her in here right now! Her contract is null! And if I have anything to say about it, she'll never record anything again." Wincing, Jim hung up and called Mrs. N.

The podcast Tamar was listening to paused and Mrs. N's picture and name popped up on her screen. She sat up, grinned and answered the call.

"Hi Mrs. N. What's up?" Tamar said casually. "Oh, gotcha. Thank you for relaying this message. Please ask Judah to listen to the songs. I'll come down there after he's done so. Also, please tell him to check his email. There's a few pictures he should see..." Tamar said in a calm, monotone voice. Mrs. N's clipped speech had made it difficult to not snap at her, but Tamar clenched her fist and kept her tone steady.

"No ma'am, I'm not joking. Judah should check his email and listen to the songs before I opt to come down there. I haven't had a call from the studio in like three years. I have a job and other obligations. I'm not contractually bound to show up whenever he calls me. Especially if he isn't calling me to sing or work on music. Have a nice evening Mrs. N." Mrs. N cut the call with a curt 'good night, young lady'. Tamar flopped backwards on her pillow and exhaled.

"She said what? That insolent... Fine, let's see this email and hear these songs. It won't make much of a dif..." Judah trailed off as he searched for and opened Tamar's email on his phone. He stood behind Jim who was at the engineering booth with his cursor hovering over the play button on the center monitor. Judah flushed red and immediately closed the tab.

"Oh. Ah, yeah. I uh." He said as he involuntarily reopened the email and pressed his phone to his chest.

"Jim, play the songs please." Judah scrolled between pictures of himself with Tamar wearing her disguise and another with her holding the wig in hand before a mirror. Another picture showed a call log with his number on the days he'd tried to call her, thinking she was Ashley. He was jolted from his scrolling by the sound of his own singing accompanied by a unique voice that he'd first heard on the evening of the singing competition almost four years ago.

"Oh, oh dear, she's... wow." Dizziness overcame Judah and he made his way over to the sofa, sat, leaned back and soaked up the melodies of the two voices with his eyes closed.

"Jim, that's my voice." Judah said, eyes still closed.

"I'm a bit hurt you've never listened to any of my songs from back in the day."

Judah opened one eye to catch Jim shrugging while still bobbing his head to the song.

"Regardless, go ahead and produce the tracks. Reach out to her if you need more vocals. Do whatever you need to do."

Jim fist pumped the air and immediately got to work. Judah slid to the edge of the sofa and pushed himself up and out. As he retreated to his office, he took another glance at the pictures.

Well, the contract said she had to do a song with someone on the label. Well played girl, well played. Judah thought as he pushed open his office door.

Tamar lay in bed in her pajamas staring at the musical notes and song lyrics she'd pasted into her ceiling years ago as a teenager. Her heart thrummed in time to the rhythm of possibilities that lay before her. Jim's email response was still open on her dimming screen. She probably wouldn't fall asleep easily. The thought of co-producing the songs with Jim played on repeat.

'You have that ear' he'd said. He was excited to work with her. She hadn't called Raya or told her mom yet. She wanted her heart to stop racing first. The notes in the ceiling felt like they were moving. A tear streaked down the side of her face, then another.

I finally have a song. Two! I have two songs!

Farah & Simone

(Shiphrah and Puah)

"We have two potential options for the expansion of the condominium project, either we go northwest into the forested area, or we acquire the properties in this community here to the west of the city and replace them with the condo units," Lucson Heylel, the CEO of Misruton Commercial Bank said, pointing at the map being projected onto the screen. The members of the board of executives sat poised, sipping beverages or scrolling on various devices, assessing cost-benefit ratios and timelines. The hand sewn, alligator leather office chairs that lined the meranti wood table were occupied by men in tailored suits. Heylel pulled up the client listing for the Yahak Cove MC Bank in the community in question. Yahak Cove was an enclosed suburban town tucked inland, west of Sawtawn City. The bank had significant roots in the community, holding mortgages for more than seventy percent of the homes there. Nodding at the screen and motioning to Heylel, the COO, Cardiff Bell spoke up.

"The prudent option is to acquire the land west of the city and build there. Going north requires new permits and zoning and significant structural work above and below ground. The cost and time would be absurd. Based on these numbers, we'd barely make forty percent on the properties after all that expenditure. When we go west, we stand to make up to sixty-five percent." Nods and murmurs undulated through the boardroom. Heylel stroked the defined edge of his laser-treated jawline and took a closer look at the rows of house icons that represented Yahak Cove. A national highway ran parallel to the little town and into the city, making it an ideal location for a new-build.

"I concur with Mr. Bell. We hold mortgages for seventy-six percent of these properties. It should be a relatively simple and cost-effective task to foreclose, and/or repossess the holdings. All infrastructure currently in place would serve as foundational to building the condos with little cost to the project." Heylel said.

"Regional manager, Rahim Faro will spearhead the project. He has experience handling these kinds of operations. He'll ensure that we acquire that land," Cardiff said. He was typing up a brief email to Faro as he spoke. Heylel nodded and clicked to the next slide.

***

Simone Puah leaned forward, face cupped in her palms, elbows on her recently organised desk, and groaned inaudibly. The glare from her two computer screens slipped through her fingers and found her eyes. She squeezed them shut and groaned again.

Stepping back from her adjustable desk, she stretched, pushed silver-streaked red hair over her shoulder to fall onto her lower back and put on her purple rimmed glasses. As she lowered her desk to sitting position, she bit her lower lip and whispered,

"Lord, we need help on this. We can't tackle this alone." She had been staring at the screen for so long that most of the words of the email were burned into her memory. Her eyes had watered a little after a while. Whether because of the content or the fact that she had neglected blinking, she wasn't sure. Leaning with one knee supported by her chair, she opened the instant messaging app.

"Sis, are you busy?" she typed and hit send. Farah Rivers responded almost immediately.

"Busy being annoyed with the letter we just got from the board."

Smirking, Simone shoved her chair back from the desk and put her white heels on before slipping into the burgundy jacket of her pants suit.

Entirely too much dressing up, when are we going back to remote work? I miss my PJs, she thought as she walked down the hall towards Farah's office.

"Did you read this nonsense?" Farah said in greeting after Simone closed the office door behind her and took a seat in the ash grey armchair angled so that they could face each other. Farah smiled at her younger counterpart. Her satin blouse had gentle, pastel flowers blooming all over it, reminding Simone of many of the gardens across Yahak Cove. Farah's office was identical to Simone's except for the desk overflowing with random assortments of papers, the faint warm aroma of some kind of candle or another, and the walls covered in family photos. Simone rolled her eyes at Farah's screen and caught her hair up in a bun.

"I think I might need to cut this like yours; it's always in the way," Simone said, straightening her pants. Farah chuckled and tapped her desktop screen a few times. On the wall across from Simone, a projection lit up showing a document with the Misruton Commercial Bank logo at the top.

"Of course I read it, why do you think I texted you?"

Farah pursed her lips and frowned, lines spreading across her forehead below the bangs of blonde highlighted pixie haircut. She spun the wedding band on her finger as her frown deepened.

"What are they even thinking? Reduce approvals by 25%-40% in Q2? Increase interest rates for qualified applicants on loans under one million? Offer buybacks for all homes in quadrants A through G? What?" Farah read, her clipped tone and half whisper cut like a fine point pen across paper. Wincing, Simone leaned back into the chair and sighed.

Simone's stomach roiled, her mind went to the smiling, waving image of old sister Evelyn watering the flowers in her front yard with pockmarked, shaky hands. Then to the fact that her and her husband Johan were still so far from saving enough for a downpayment on their own home.

"We're not doing it, are we?" she asked, swallowing the lump in her throat and rubbing her thighs both to smooth the wrinkles from her pants and to keep her legs from shaking. Farah shook her head violently, gnawing her lower lip and drumming her fingers on the desk.

"Definitely not. We just have to figure out how to navigate it."

Farah's brows furrowed as she drummed on the desk more fervently. Nodding, Simone pulled her phone from her pocket.

"I think I have an idea; I read through the document four times to be sure. But the pre-approval process was not mentioned." Simone said softly, maintaining the hushed tone that had taken over the room. Farah's fingers stopped moving as she turned to her friend, smiling.

"The computer pre-approves applicants based on preset criteria." Farah said, no longer chewing her lip. Simone, grinning, nodded.

Farah straightened and tapped at the keyboard before her. On the projected screen, the words no result popped up in the search bar five times after she had tried various terms.

"You're right girl! There's nothing in here about pre-approval, early approval, changing the approval parameters or anything," Farah declared.

"They wanted to avoid saying it outright in case we get audited," Simone said.

"They're expecting fear to get brokers to do the dirty work," Farah said, Simone straightened in the armchair and clenched her fists.

"Well, I don't fear them, or anyone else, so they can stuff it. And they can keep the year-end bonus. If we do this, that's blood money."

"Exactly," Farah was nodding. She ran her hands through her hair a few times and pouted.

"Talking 'bout reduced approvals," Simone continued, rolling her eyes. "How are people gonna get houses?"

She threw her hands into the air and shook her head. Farah mirrored the action.

"That's what I'm saying! Anyways girl, what are we going to do about the interest rate increase?" Farah asked. Simone's hands dropped and her shoulders sagged.

"I don't know, most folks don't qualify for a million."

They sat in silence for fifteen minutes before Farah spoke again.

"How's about we pray on this part?" she said, there were crow's feet peeking out under her lightly done makeup. Simone sighed. Farah hadn't taken a vacation in more years than Simone was willing to count.

"I have paperwork up to my nose and I have to prep something to say to the team, so they don't do this foolishness to people just trying to survive," Farah said. Simone nodded and rose, heading for the door.

"Be careful how you word it to them though, someone might try to kiss up. Wait, actually, don't say anything other than that you want final decisions to go through you. That way you can batch approve everyone who has pre-approval." Simone said over her shoulder.

"Yeah girl, that's wisdom. This is why they pay you the big bucks," Farah said.

Laughing, Simone let herself out and walked back to her office. A thought hit her, and she turned on her heels and popped her head back into Farah's office.

"Actually, we have to tell the brokers—maybe not all of them—but they'd get blindsided if Corporate asks why they haven't hit the quotas," she said, still whispering.

"When you say not all of them, are you talking about who I think you're talking about?" Farah said, tilting her head to one side. A frown formed, half hidden under her bangs. She sipped coffee from the canister Simone had gotten her for Mothers' Day.

"Yeah, I am," Simone replied.

"Well, we've been meaning to invite her for a BBQ anyways, now we really have a reason. We should've done this months ago," Farah said, making a note in the white planner that she never went anywhere without. Simone smiled softly, Johan had bought Farah the planner for Christmas. He'd bought her one every Christmas for a very long time.

"I mean, she came in when we were pretty busy with the refurbishing projects and the apartment building, and she doesn't really talk to anyone," Simone said.

"True, but you gotta be friendly to make friends and we're the ones who want to reach her, not the other way around," Farah said, closing the planner and looking back up at Simone. Nodding acquiescence, Simone left and returned to her own desk.

She's not originally from here but Farah is right, we should've made her feel at home here, like part of the family. All we did was a fruit basket and a small intro meeting. That's entirely not enough. I guess Johan is firing up the grill, he'll be happy about that. Oh, I need to design invites and check if she's vegan.

***

The Yahak Cove MCB branch had a total of twenty employees, four of whom handled loans and credit. Farah, as branch manager, met with each of the loan agents under the guise of one-on-one improvement meetings. As was the case in every business place in Yahak Cove, most of the staff of the MCB were born and raised there. The town—partially enclosed by untouched woodlands—was home to people from myriad backgrounds whose great-great grandparents had moved from other parts of the country or overseas seeking work in the blooming city. Half of the two hundred and forty residents commuted to the city for work every day. The other half staffed the elementary, middle and high schools, the one bank, the single church, the clinic, and the miscellaneous stores on the strip mall. Yahak Cove, like a few other small towns whose residents flowed into Sawtawn, had been built by settlers over a hundred years prior.

When Farah called the 'city girl' loan agent, Emily, who had started in the branch less than a year prior, she wasn't sure how she'd even approach the conversation. Eventually, she resigned to simply doing an actual performance review and to invite Emily to a barbeque. Farah almost turned into a puddle in her chair when Emily's face lit up and she readily agreed to coming over for the barbeque.

"That sounds amazing! To be honest, I'm really glad you called us in for these reviews. Now that my probation is up, I really wanted to get to know some people better. I was super scared to talk to anyone. Is everyone from the branch coming?" Emily asked, words spilling out of her mouth. She was abuzz with palpable excitement. Farah shuddered. Feeding twenty people, plus their families meant a huge get-together and an even huger budget.

"Uh, no. Only the loans team and the assistant branch manager," Farah said quickly to prune expectations.

"Oh!" Emily said, still beaming. "That's fine too, can my partner come as well?"

"I don't see why not!" Farah said, sighing deeply. *Thank God, because I definitely wasn't feeding all those people out of pocket.*

Emily thanked her again for inviting her, shook Farah's hand and left the office almost skipping.

The three other loan agents were third and fourth generation residents and immediately agreed to do whatever they could to protect their neighbours' assets.

"They want us to offer buybacks? Some of these houses have been in these families forever. They're legacy homes. Family homes. What on earth are they planning? I'm hearing rumors about condos or something," said Rachel, a woman close to Farah's age who'd spent her whole life in Yahak Cove and knew just about everyone by name. She was frowning as she pushed her salt and pepper tresses out of her face for the fifth time.

"Don't worry about the gossip and rumors. It doesn't matter what they have planned, as long as we don't force our friends and neighbours out of their homes it won't matter." Farah said, glad she had no hair to hang in her face.

"True, anyways, have a good weekend. I won't be pushing any bloody buybacks on hard-working people who just want to live where they were born. Do these board members even know how hard it was to even qualify for these homes fifty years ago? My dad worked twelve- hour days while my mom sewed and sold dresses for twenty-one years before they had enough saved. She had carpal tunnel syndrome by the time she was done, and my dad's arthritis is so bad that he can't stand for more than a few minutes at a time and he's not even seventy yet," Rachel said in one breath. Her fists were clenched so tightly that Farah almost reached across her desk and held her hand.

Farah sucked in air through her lips and blew out slowly. Rachel was right, Yahak Cove was full of people who had fought for homeownership.

"You're not wrong Rachel, not at all. It's evil. I couldn't look anyone in the eye at the supermarket if we did this. Enjoy your weekend, say hi to Rael for me."

As Rachel left, Farah slumped in her chair, instantly losing the straight-backed posture she tried to hold in front of her staff. Her neck was stiff, and her heart raced every time she looked at the signature at the bottom of the letter. If MCB fired her, how would she afford rent.

Jerry, I miss you. Why'd you have to go and leave me alone? Lord, why'd you have to take him so early? Eleven years of marriage and I have nothing to show for it except a ring, a grave and a pile of debts that I've barely paid off. She thought as she absentmindedly shuffled papers around on her desk. When the papers were stacked as neatly as she could manage while not looking at them, her right hand immediately found her ring finger, and she began rotating the ring repeatedly. Losing her husband in her early forties after spending their savings trying to keep him alive had given her alopecia and grey hair in one go. Farah felt tears she'd cried too many times brimming in the corners of her eyes. Rubbing her neck, she booted up her computer and got back to work.

"Thank you for coming in, please have a seat, both of you," Simone said, gesturing to the two heather grey armchairs placed before her desk. She'd straightened the desk, and the office, ten times that day already, after every client. They didn't need to see her desk looking like how her brain felt most of the time. The middle-aged couple both took a seat, the wife first, as the husband held her hand and made sure she was comfortable. Simone smiled, remembering the first time Johan held her hand as they walked through the park late one evening. His eyes had been darting from area to area, leaving her wondering if he was paying her any attention. Then he'd immediately held her hand as some cyclists zipped by.

"Sorry, I didn't mean to be forceful. My sister said it's more dangerous out at night for women than most men realise. I guess I'm a little paranoid."

She'd felt a flutter in her chest from before that night and that flutter bloomed into full blown warmth in that moment.

"Thank you for seeing us Mrs. Puah. We won't take up too much of your time," the woman, Martha Anderson said as Simone took her own seat.

"No worries Mrs. Anderson, you can take your time here. At MCB, we're here to serve." Simone felt the tackiness of the lie on her tongue. Well, not a lie per se. Her and many of the staff truly cared to serve their community but MCB only served the Heylel Group of companies. They only served money.

Martha was wringing her hands together and Thomas was clenching and unclenching his fists, they glanced at each other and sighed. Thomas looked down for a moment then hit Simone with an intense stare.

"Our daughter got into a university on the west coast. A prestigious one that gives her a real shot at a future. She's the first person in my family who has a chance to go that far." Thomas said, his jaw was set like a cinder block and his eyes, for a moment, burned Simone with their intensity. Martha smiled, her eyes wet with unshed tears. Simone, intrigued, leaned slightly forward in her chair then quickly adjusted when she remembered what her role in this conversation was.

"I see," Simone said, swallowing the curious inflection threatening to peek through in her voice.

"Hearty congratulations to your daughter and to you both for doing a great job supporting her to this point," she added. Thomas smiled and nodded but Martha's chin fell, and she stared at her lap.

"Thank you. She has worked very hard." Martha responded, barely above a whisper.

"She truly has," Thomas continued.

"We are here to refinance our home or use it as some kind of asset to get a loan to pay her tuition. We aren't sure how it all works."

"Ah, I see. I understand." Simone said, her hands moved to her keyboard and mouse as she spoke.

"Please give me one moment to pull up the details of your mortgage and banking information." A sensation whirled around in Simone's body. Something like a presence resting on her. Gentle but strong. Comforting. Nodding to herself, she accessed their accounts and began to scroll through.

"Apologies Mr. and Mrs. Anderson, I am seeing here that you've had some challenges in the past with maintaining consistent payments. At the moment, you've gone beyond the given repayment term. We do not currently have the ability to refinance your home." Simone steeled herself and kept her face neutral. Martha was squeezing Thomas' hand; his steely gaze had melted away in tears held in his eyes by pure will.

"I must also advise you that your home is rather close to being considered for foreclosure due to missed payments." Simone's countenance strained under the false straight face she was showing. This part of the job made her wish she'd taken up accounting instead of financial management. When the numbers became people's lives, it felt like she was trapped in an elevator by herself, with the power cut off and no cell service. The lingering presence hovering around her slowly swept away the knots in her stomach as she watched Martha wring her hands and Thomas open and close his mouth over and over, just staring at her. Simone's own burgeoning tears flavoured her mouth with bitterness and tugged at the corners of her eyes.

"I am going to be completely transparent with you both. The state of your accounts does not give you much room to access loan products or lines of credit either." Simone said. She swallowed the bitterness in her mouth and leaned into the simultaneous peace enveloping her.

"We know, we checked the accounts online. Paying bills has been brutal because I got really sick and couldn't work for a year." Thomas said through gritted teeth.

"It's not just you dear. I don't earn enough, I never have." Martha added, her head fully hung. Simone could reach out and touch the weight settling into the room.

"I'm sorry to hear that finances have been so difficult for you both. Not having stable income in this economy makes things even more difficult than they are for most people. A friend of mine has a 'prestigious' position," Simone said using air quotes. "But she still has a hard time making ends meet because of things outside of her control."

Thomas squeezed Martha's hand gently, her head was still bowed, her shoulders slumped. After three silent, deep breaths, Simone rolled her neck and threw on a large smile.

"That's the bad news, not much we can do about what's already happened. The good news is that there are many scholarships for this community specifically. They are based on grades and/or need. Your daughter likely already qualifies. What's her name? I don't think you mentioned it." Simone said, Thomas' eyes brightened, and Martha sat up and met Simone's gaze for the first time since they'd sat down.

"Chloe." Came the response in chorus.

"Beautiful name." Simone said, waiting to allow Thomas's shoulders to relax and Martha to sit back in the chair.

"Well, if Chloe can get into a prestigious school, then she's likely qualified for one or more scholarships from Ayden

Farms. Many people don't know unless they're actively looking, but the Farms support our community heavily. They also have a debt consolidation grant that could remove a significant portion of your debt if you present your case to them." Simone said, relishing the ease with which these words were flowing. Representatives from Ayden had approached her and Farah years before, letting them know that the organization had a vested interest in Yahak Cove—Simone was never told why—and that they'd support where they could. Recently, they'd covered costs for renovations to the schools and church.

Slack jawed, the couple stared at her as she handed them two brochures. As they read, their eyes grew wider and wider. They read, stared at each other, read some more. Thomas was shaking his head and Martha was openly weeping by the time they finished browsing the monochrome brochures about Ayden Farms financial support services.

"Who are these people? No one gives away money like that," Thomas said finally.

"Actually, that's not true. There are quite a few millionaires and this one billionaire who targets communities like ours to help them in subtle but impactful ways. Most recipients sign nondisclosure agreements to keep masses of people from rushing to get help they don't need, but the organization does help many. I know because they paid my full tuition and room and board when I was going to college. They even paid for my Masters' degree." Simone said. She sighed as discreetly as she could. Her and Johan might not own a home, but neither of them was in debt thanks to Ayden Farms.

"If they have an NDA, will you get in trouble for telling us about them?" Martha asked, wiping her eyes with a paper napkin that Simone had handed her.

"No, each recipient gets one recommendation they can give out."

"One?" Martha asked, her stare wider than before.

"For your whole life you can only talk about it once?" Thomas asked, his head tilted. Simone chuckled and nodded.

"And you chose us?"

The tears in Martha's eyes broke free again and ran down her flushed cheeks. Thomas' lips were quivering; his eyes shimmered with tears resting on his lower eyelid.

"There is a significant process you have to go through, and Chloe will have to work on the farm or in the factory each summer until she finishes her degree but yes, I feel led to tell you about this opportunity," Simone said and sighed as the presence lifted, and the room started to feel like she could breathe again. The peace remained, and she leaned back into her chair just enough to take the pressure off her neck and shoulders. The sensation of being urged on had dissipated, leaving her with a sureness that she hadn't felt since saying yes to Johan.

So that's what that feels like? Neat, I gotta tell Johan. Thanks, Holy Spirit, that was cool.

"We'll do whatever it takes. Thank God and thank you! You have no idea what you're doing for our family," Thomas said, individual tears streaked his cheek. He wiped them quickly and cleared his throat. Martha was still staring at Simone, alternating between shaking her head and nodding.

***

"We need to find a way to increase the financial literacy in YC asap! Our people have no idea how any of this works and honestly, it's a miracle that we haven't seen anyone yet who we outright had to foreclose on."

Simone was sitting on Farah's couch eating rum and raisin ice cream with a fork.

"We can't be the ones to teach them though. Neither of us can afford to get fired," Farah said, shaking her head, Simone groaned.

"Get fired for what?" Simone asked, rolling her eyes.

"We wouldn't be sharing company secrets or anything. It's all common knowledge. Folks just don't know what to look for or how to understand it all."

"They'd find a reason. And they'd figure we've been helping people avoid buyouts and foreclosures." Farah said, taking a sip of the box-wine, she was nursing. She spun her wedding band with her thumb as she clutched the wine glass with her right hand. Simone winced. The image of the Andersons smiling just barely held at bay the dread of what management would say if they took a close look at how easy it would've been to foreclose on that family's home. Shuddering, she shoved a big scoop of ice cream into her mouth and let the cramping of her soft palate distract her from the way her heartbeat sped up every time she thought about it.

If Farah and I ever get audited... whew Jesus. Simone thought as she shoved more ice cream into her mouth and pulled her legs up into the couch.

The sounds of ice cream being scooped and snatched from the fork filled the evening chorus, forming an erratic harmony with the TV that neither of them was watching and the cicadas somewhere beyond the glass door that led to the apartment balcony. Simone preferred Farah's company to the droning silence of the four walls of her and Johan's apartment on the weeks when he worked nights at his second job. No matter how many devices she ran simultaneously, the silence pressed in like a dull ache. Usually, invading ideas plagued her until exhaustion dropped her into sleep. On the walls and ceiling danced images of him driving the shuttle bus with red rimmed, bloodshot eyes, running on coffee and prayer. And pray as she might, the thoughts wouldn't leave her. So, Farah's apartment it was.

The conversations and ice cream and random discussions about Scripture kept her mind occupied until she was comfortably tired enough to saunter back to her own apartment, shower and pass out on the couch. The bedroom unnerved her without Johan there. Sleeping beside him over three years to then not have his warmth for half the week was jarring.

Stupid house prices. Why do we need a house anyways? She thought, shivering as she reached for more ice cream. Johan was bent on them owning a home.

"You can't be a banker, and live in an apartment, that's just... I don't know, I want our kids to have a backyard and a treehouse or something." He'd said when he'd brought up driving part-time. She hated seeing him so tired that he was essentially sleepwalking through weekends.

"Okay, so we need a third party to teach them." Farah offered. Simone shook herself from the images that should have stayed in her apartment and turned to look at Farah who had drained her glass and was now on her phone, searching for potential financial educators.

"A third party they won't ignore and one that won't charge stupid prices for a 'life changing course' and then spew rubbish about cryptocurrency for two hours." Simone said. Farah rolled her eyes.

"Agreed. Ew."

"Okay, so church is the easiest way to get most people to show up. Everyone loves Pastor Aaron," Farah said, reaching for her planner and pen from the coffee table. Simone nodded.

"We can recommend some people, and he can reach out and bring them in." Farah continued.

"Yeah good. But what about the people who are already in debt?" Simone asked, the ice cream was not working at all, her thoughts were running.

"We are those people," Farah said, shrugging. "That part is bigger than us."

The grounds of the church were teeming with people. Men with canes and walkers mingled with teenagers and young adults leaned up against cars or sitting on the grass. A gentle autumn drift pirouetted leaves through the crowd of more than a hundred people present for day two of the 'Stewardship Conference.' Simone and Farah had both rolled their eyes at the name but figured it wouldn't raise any warning bells for the MCB leadership.

"Why are they calling it a conference?" Emily asked, sipping on an iced lemonade from the stand that was being run by the children's church third grade class. Fresh lemons had been picked from the farms that ran adjacent to the forest and bordered Yahak Cove to the far south-west.

"Because," Farah groaned, "everything is a conference." She made another blatant show of rolling her eyes.

"It's a church thing. Fancy titles and all that old, traditional stuff that makes things sound grander than they are," Simone said. Emily shrugged and walked over to the MCB booth that they'd been instructed to set up.

"Still don't know why we have to advertise MCB here," Simone said. She and Farah turned to go find pastor Aaron who had scheduled ten financial professionals, all willing to show up for free. He stood cracking jokes with the two people who would be presenting that day. The first was an older lady, a financier from Ayden Farms who would also make a whole semester of classes available online at no cost. She'd been with Ayden Farms for longer than Simone had been alive. The second was a millionaire from Ethiopia who pastor Aaron had met years ago on a mission trip to the Middle East. In his twenties, the Ethiopian had turned a business in his village into a sustainable franchise that spread across the country.

"Hi pastor," Farah and Simone said in unison.

"Hello, glad you both came over before we get into the swing of things," Pastor Aaron said before patting both the financier and the millionaire on their shoulders and beckoning to the pair of bankers to follow him.

"We have something for you both," he said. Farah and Simone shared a look. Pastor Aaron led them to a table covered with gift cards, baskets, and boxes. A bunch of people from the community were standing behind and on either side of the table.

"THANK YOU, FARAH AND SIMONE," They yelled in unison. Farah immediately started crying. She squeezed Simone's hand and used her other hand to cover her mouth. Simone let the tears run over her no smudge makeup and down her chin.

"We wanted to thank you for putting on this event, for saving many of our homes and for taking the time to actually listen to people who come into the bank," Pastor Aaron said to a chorus of raucous applause.

"We had no idea what we were doing with our money!" Someone yelled from the crowd. Before Simone could place the voice, the crowd started cheering again. Pastor Aaron walked over and hugged them both, patting them on the back. The gathering followed suit and proceeded to hug, thank and share stories family by family with Simone and Farah for the next hour until the speakers were ready to start presenting on the podium that had been constructed in the church parking lot. Simone could barely maintain her composure when Chloe Anderson walked up and gave her the biggest hug. Chloe had already spoken to the scholarship committee at Ayden Farms and was pre-approved. By the time the speakers were ready to go, Farah was exhausted and had to retreat to her car. Simone sat in the church building with Johan, her head on his shoulder, tears drying on her cheeks.

"You both deserve every gift and every word you heard today. You're the best bankers this town could ever hope for," Johan whispered. Simone nudged him with her shoulder.

"Shhh, I've cried enough, thanks."

As the event ended, Simone and Johan made their way out to beat the crowd leaving the church yard. Simone turned to wave goodbye to Emily. With her arm aloft and mid-wave, she froze and became deathly pale. Their MCB regional manager was standing beside Emily, scowling.

***

Six months later, Farah and Simone sat in Simone's office staring at their phones but not really paying attention to what was on the screens. They'd just come out of a short, sharp meeting with Rahim Faro, regional manager of MCB branches in Yahak Cove, Sawtawn City and other surrounding towns in Misruton. The edge on his words still rang in Simone's ears. His frigid glare toward the team had made Emily cry. Simone frowned. Emily's exuberance since the barbeque had been so refreshing. Every few weeks the aroma of her baked delights filled the entire branch. She'd even gone to Farah on her own to say that she didn't feel comfortable foreclosing homes to hit a metric. When she'd told Farah "I came into banking to put people into homes, not to take them out."

Simone had wanted to hug her and do a little jig. She could only hope that Emily's spirit wasn't broken and that she wouldn't decide to pivot and cave into Rahim and MCB's demands. He'd been lingering around the branch since the Stewardship Conference, and his scowl had become a permanent fixture and a source of dread in the branch.

The rate of mortgage approvals had increased by almost the exact percentage he'd instructed them to reduce it by. Less than ten foreclosures had taken place in the almost one year since they'd been sent that first email from the head office. Rahim had called meetings with every broker in the bank, the management team, and Farah as head of the branch.

They'd all been silent as he lobbed searing questions at them about what was happening.

"The clients all meet the criteria for whatever they come in for. And the ones who had arrears all found ways to pay off or manage their debts," was all Farah had managed to whisper. Her throat had been so dry, she nearly had a coughing fit when Rahim stalked from the board room.

That man. Simone thought as she absentmindedly thumbed through her app menu.

"Rahim Faro is awful," she whispered. Farah nodded and stretched. Her sea foam floral boat neck blouse shimmered.

"I hope I never have to talk with him again," Farah said before rising to leave.

"Agreed, my stomach still hurts."

As Simone continued to scroll through the apps, she clicked on the period tracker without really thinking about it. As her vision slowly came into focus, realization seeped into body, causing her to start to sweat under the crisp air conditioning. Her period was almost three weeks late. With all the meetings and filing and preparation the staff team had needed for Rahim's arrival, she hadn't really paid attention to her cycle. Plus, it usually had a mind of its own anyways.

I can't be pregnant though. With the fibroids and everything else, they were sure my chances were slim. I'm not even gonna buy the test to check it. It'll show up in a few days. Has it ever been this late though? She said to herself while checking what time Sam's pharmacy closed.

I don't need a pregnancy test, do I? Three weeks is a long time.

Simone spent the rest of the afternoon pacing her office, caught between conflicting thoughts. If she checked and she wasn't pregnant, she wouldn't know how to feel. If she was pregnant, she wanted to know right away. They'd tried for so long that they'd given up. Johan had apologised four of five times for asking her if she wanted to try again for a baby. Each time, he'd be watching something or see kids playing and blurt it out before thinking about it. Then he'd hug her tight and tell her that he was sorry for bringing it up again. He'd even gone to test his sperm to see if it was him.

My sweet silly man. She thought as she raised her desk to a standing position and focused on getting some work done before the day ended.

She wanted to know.

As soon as they left work, she rerouted Farah to Sam's and bought three different tests while Farah browsed in random aisles.

"I didn't even realise you were at the cashier until I heard Sam talking to you." Farah said when they got back to the car, looking over at Simone who was staring straight ahead.

"What's up?" she asked. Simone squeezed her purse in her lap and didn't look her friend's way.

"I just got feminine products, that's all."

"Oh, hmmm. I'm gonna chalk up you acting weird to the fact that Rahim made everyone want to quit today," Farah said, chuckling. Simone mustered a weak laugh and drummed up conversation about Rahim and the financial literacy classes at the church. Farah fell into the conversation which lasted until they arrived at the apartment complex. Feigning the need to pee, Simone sped off to her apartment, leaving a confused Farah standing at her own door with her keys in her hand.

"She couldn't pee here like she always does? Johan isn't even home. Eh, whatever. She'll call me later." Farah said to herself before entering her apartment.

All three tests came back positive.

"Thank you, Jesus." Simone whispered. Tears rolled down her face as she lost strength in her knees and was glad that she was already on the toilet. A half an hour later, she texted Johan, not wanting to call while he was driving. Her mom was her next call, followed by Farah. In twenty minutes, both were in her apartment. Farah had gone to pick up Simone's mom at the other end of Yahak Cove and they'd driven back together.

Simone was trembling with more feelings than she knew what to do with. Johan wouldn't see his phone until his break later that night, but she knew he'd likely rush home the moment he read the message. Her mom and Farah meanwhile were talking up a storm on the couch beside her. She barely heard anything they said as her mind swam in thought.

"We should buy a house together. Neither of us will be able to do it alone and you'll need help with the baby," Farah said, nudging her back to the moment.

"What?" Simone asked.

"We should buy a house together. You've been saving, I've been saving. We could get there together long before the baby is born." Simone's mom was grinning and nodding. Farah was beaming in that way she did when things worked out for people. Thoughts bounced like a dozen pinballs in Simone's head. Farah nudged her with her elbow.

"Uh, let's wait until Johan and I talk about things. I won't decide that on my own." Farah nodded and continued talking to Mrs. Lewis without missing a beat.

Johan's face was streaming tears when she opened the door to meet him later that night. His text response had been quick, "I'm coming home asap. I love you." He scooped her up into his arms and kissed her face and neck while the tears continued. He immediately agreed with Farah's idea to buy a house together and was overjoyed to have support.

"Babies are scary and hard to take care of," he said. He hadn't let go of Simone since he'd picked her up at the door. She was currently sitting in his lap with her legs stretched out into the sofa.

"Farah is amazing, so is your mom. Plus, my mom can always come by and help too. It's great. I'm excited. Can you tell I'm excited? How are you feeling about all this?" Johan said. Simone chuckled and kissed him.

"Excited. Scared, uh... overwhelmed is a good word too," Simone replied. When Johan had picked her up, his heart had been racing, and his breaths came short. He'd since calmed down for the most part, but his eyes told the story of a mind running full speed.

Four hours later, Simone smiled at a nodding Johan who was falling asleep mid-sentence and slurring his words. With what energy she had left, she slid off his lap, put a cushion behind his head and snuggled up beside him. She dozed off with the dawn peeking through the window to thoughts of a baby giggling as Johan blew raspberries on their tummy.

***

Rahim Faro slammed his fist on his desk and grabbed a pair of boxing gloves from beside a golden trophy he'd won for being top regional manager five years in a row. He hurled his fist into the body opponent bag in the corner of his office. The twenty-fifth storey suite-cum-office had wrap-around glass walls with unidirectional tinting. It sat in the middle of the Heylel group building which also housed one of the main MCB branches on the ground floor. Untouched, custom leather furniture was the only audience as Rahim punished the punching bag for the failure of the Yahak Cove MCB in what he knew to be a simple task.

"Those detestable women," he said as a right hook set the punching bag off-kilter.

"They protected those stupid people. How are they still putting up good numbers in that crab-hole town?" he said between breaths. His face was beet red twenty minutes later when he yanked off the gloves and launched them across the room where they connected with the shatterproof windows with a dull thud.

"Ayden Farms Group is helping them. Everywhere we turn, that infernal corporation is cutting our profits with their confounded philanthropy!"

A month later, Ramon stood in the center of the main floor of the Yahak Cove MCB branch to address the staff one Monday morning before the branch opened.

"Farah Rivers is no longer employed with our organization," he said.

Simone was still trembling. Farah had forced her to come to work after receiving the termination email that Friday. Simone felt ill. Farah was in her apartment drinking box wine and watching reruns.

"God will provide something else. My résumé is amazing," was all Farah had said after telling Simone that she needed to go to work because they couldn't both be out of a job, especially since Simone was pregnant.

"For the foreseeable future, until this branch begins to meet the organization's targets, I will oversee operations as the branch manager. I will have meetings with each of you to determine how each department will meet the goals we have developed for you all. That is all," Rahim said, he turned down the hall, up the stairs in the direction of what used to be Farah's office. It had already been cleaned out and the contents delivered to her apartment the day before. Simone gagged. The letter had said some corporate garbage about consistently falling below metrics, and the need for restructuring to remain profitable.

"You mean to sustain your greed," Simone said under her breath as she made her way towards her own office. As she passed Emily, she sighed. The young lady was as pale as printer paper. Simone closed her office door after staring down the hall she'd walked hundreds of times just to chat with Farah. As a senior member of the branch, she'd be called into that office eventually.

"If you ask me to do some shady stuff to get people out of their homes, I'm not doing it. You can good and well fire me," she said as she slumped into her chair. Rubbing her tummy, she looked at the staff pictures on her wall from the barbeques and other events Farah had held over the years. Simone shook away tears and dug into her work.

***

Simone's first trimester was both the most beautiful and scariest three months of her life. All her checkups with the gynecologist went smoothly. But the morning sickness forced her to work a hybrid schedule so that she wasn't always running to the bathroom at work. Ranon Faro had approved it within minutes of her sending the request to his email.

"Of course he wants me out," she said to Johan as he rubbed her back and held hair in their bathroom. She dry-heaved a few times until it was clear she had nothing else to throw up.

"He wants a free run at the branch. Lord, help us."

Johan had to leave in a few minutes to go back out. He had taken on even more hours to save the final amounts they would need for the downpayment on a house. Farah had started teaching online classes at a college in the city to earn some extra money as well. Between severance from over twenty years at MCB and a government stipend from being unemployed, she had a shadow of her MCB income. The online classes in accounting and financial management had been oversubscribed, causing her to get more sessions than the college had originally planned for. Farah was getting paid, but teaching back-to-back classes daily and marking assignments had left her worn out. Both Farah and Johan milled around Simone on the weekends with blackened bags under red eyes and groaning of shoulder and back pains. Every dollar they could spare went into the house downpayment account they started together.

One Saturday morning, Simone lay on her sofa, rubbing her tummy and reading a novel. Farah was teaching a class and Johan was out buying groceries. When her phone vibrated, lit up and showed the email icon, she rolled her eyes. Forty minutes later, she rolled out of the sofa, straightened Johan's hoodie that she was borrowing and went to use the restroom. As she stood at the sink washing her hands, the front door of the apartment opened, and Johan crab walked in with grocery bags hanging from every part of his arms and torso.

"Babe?" Simone said when she came out of the bathroom. Johan ambled over to the counter that divided the kitchen and the living area and heaved half the bags off his arm.

"Never making two trips," he said between breaths. He swung another set of bags onto the counters and threw down the remaining ones on the floor next to the fridge. Simone rolled her eyes, rubbed his arms, and began to put items into the fridge.

"Did you see the email from building management?" he said suddenly, his expression darkening. Simone froze with a tray of eggs in her hand.

"I got an email, but I thought it was work or spam so... what did it say?" Simone answered, closing the fridge after sliding the tray onto the top shelf.

"Those a-holes are evicting all tenants in two months," he said through gritted teeth. Simone paled. Thoughts crashed into her mind in torrents.

Where will we live? Where will Farah live? What are they gonna do with the building? Do we have enough to find a house? Is there even a house available?

Nausea gripped her, leaving her swaying. Dizzy, she made her way back to the couch while Johan continued to unpack groceries.

"Are you okay hun? Would you like some water or something?" he asked, concern melting through the anger. She shook her head and smiled weakly. He paused and walked over to her, moving hair from her face and kissing her forehead.

"First Farah, now this? What is happening?"

***

Simone was relieved when—two weeks before the apartment was due to be closed—they found some retirees moving out of the country who were willing to sell them a house at a steal.

"You two did too much for this community for us to even consider asking full price," the old man had said when asked if he and his wife were sure about the final offer. With the amount they were asking, Farah, Simone and Johan already had enough saved for the downpayment and easily qualified for the mortgage. The couple who sold the house flew out a month later, leaving all their furniture and appliances behind.

"I don't think I can cry anymore," Farah said as they stood watching some of the young men of the community move their luggage and other belongings into their new home. Simone could only smile and rub her tummy while also rubbing her friend's back. Farah was spinning her wedding band around on her finger, biting her lip and overtly holding back tears. The forty-year-old home on the west end of the town, near to the forest and the farms had four bedrooms, two stories with a back patio leading out to a quaint garden and burnt sienna roof that had recently been replaced.

"We have to put solar panels in when we can manage to save up the money," Simone said to Farah, who was occasionally looking up to the sky and shaking her head.

"Jerry should be here to see this," Farah whispered, Simone pulled her friend by her waist into a hug.

"I can't imagine how much you miss him. He would have loved this," Simone said.

"He would have loved you. He always told Johan to marry a nice girl so that he could get grandnephews and grandnieces. I don't know why that man always talked like he was so old."

Farah's voice quivered and cracked.

"We were so young when he was taken away from me. Now I'm old and by myself," she added. Simone hugged her tighter, ignoring the pang of guilt as they watched Johan and a young man tilt a bookshelf and shimmy their way through the front door.

"I'm so sorry he's gone, Farah. Stupid cancer," Simone grumbled. Farah looked across at her and smiled weakly.

"It's not okay, but it's okay. I have you and Johan and my god-baby on the way. I miss him, but I haven't been lonely in years," Farah said, returning the hug.

As they settled into their new home on one end of Yahak Cove, people who lived on the easternmost side, closer to the city, met the full brunt of the Heylel Group's influence. Less than four months after Rahim's first visit to the Cove, more than half the people in that section of the community lost their jobs in the city, had the legality of their homeownership contested and overturned or were outright threatened to move out or risk losing their livelihood. The group of companies was rumoured to have called in favours from every business place in the city that employed Yahak Cove residents. There was, of course, no proof. Only conjecture and an undercurrent of dread that seeped into the small town and sent shivers down Simone's spine. She still had her job at MCB but was now under the crushing palm of a wage freeze, hiring freeze, reduced staff, and external auditors who had essentially moved into the office beside Rahim's. The atmosphere in the branch went frigid. No more chats over coffee and Emily showing up with freshly baked pies for all to share. Everyone—including Simone, who had half a closet of vibrant colours—was relegated to the drab gold and beige company pants suits and plain brown or navy shoes. Rahim walked the halls of the branch and peered in when agents were with clients. He personally took any case where the client owned a home on the east side. Simone felt ill anytime someone walked past her office towards his. They'd usually leave weeping or swearing. After the first week of it, Simone left her door closed when she was in the office.

By the middle of Simone's pregnancy, the eastern section of Yahak Cove was empty of residents who were either forced into apartment complexes—most of which were owned by the Heylel group—in the city or moved in with relatives in the remaining portion of the Cove. By month eight of her term, she was waddling into work because she was no longer allowed to work from home. Half of the town was empty of original homeowners and demolition had begun.

"Well, I guess the condos aren't a rumor anymore," Emily said to Simone as they walked to the parking lot. Farah was waiting for Simone in her car, as she'd done since being fired. Demolition cranes were visible from the branch in the middle of town. The plumes of dust had relegated Simone and anyone with certain medical complications to wear masks whenever they were outside. Simone sighed and rested her hand under her belly.

"I can't believe they tore down the apartments too. They owned it," Emily continued.

"I'm sure they want to tear down the whole town, Em," Simone said as they reached Farah's car. Emily's purple electric scooter was parked next to the grey compact sedan with a floral decal across the rear bumper.

"I'm going home to my knitting. I'm tired of talking about MCB and the Heylel Group. Tired," Simone said. Emily grumbled about starting a pie bakery so that she could quit and Simone shrugged before working her way into the car.

"Ugh," she said when she had finally sat down. Through the half open passenger door, she smiled weakly at Emily who was now on her scooter wearing a fuchsia helmet and matching jacket.

"Ayden Farms Group might be interested in your pies. As for those folks? I'm just glad they aren't eating up the whole town."

Barbara

(Rahab)

A second pair of men knocked at Barbara's door. Usually, the men and women who passed through her building stayed on the lower floors. Even through the peephole in the door, it was clear they weren't here for entertainment. These two made their presence known with heavy bangs that rattled the condo. Barbara's parents stared wide eyed at her, covering their mouths, then quickly averted their gazes when she reapplied her lipstick, her customer-facing smile and a straight-backed posture and opened the door wide. With one hand on her hip, she allowed her body to form an alluring silhouette in the door with the lights illuminating her curves from behind. The parts of her body not cast in shadow revealed a low-cut red dress, soft, heavy auburn curls cascading down her neck and a bright, white smile.

"Hello fellas, how can we be of service this evening?" she said, melody weaving her words in their direction. The men barely fit on the landing of the narrow stairwell that led up to where Barbara and her family stayed on the third floor. Broad shoulders, hard-set frowns, and piercing gazes greeted her and rejected her cordial salutation. They fanned her off and stomped their way across the threshold.

"We know they came through here!" said the taller man, Jerick. His threaded eyebrows furrowed as his eyelids narrowed, snake-like. He wore a khaki tank top that was two sizes two small and camouflage cargo pants with a pocket every few inches.

"Where are they? Where are the pigs? We know they came in here," Jerrick continued, he tore the room apart with his stare, peering around every corner and into every room as he circled the hallway and living area that he and his counterpart had stepped into.

"Evening, Mr. and Mrs. Waldron," the other man said. That was Cory, only shorter than Jerick by a few inches. He turned his bulky frame towards Barbara's parents and smiled with uncomfortably white teeth in a way that made both the seniors flinch. Her parents were huddled together in one corner of the sofa chaise as far from the front door as they could manage. The two men made the spacious living area claustrophobic. The back of Barbara's neck prickled, she quickly placed herself between them, holding her trademark smile in place and straightening her back further to redirect the attention of the two men.

Then they brandished the handguns, both of which were longer than a person's forearm. Behind her, her mother whimpered, her father mumbled what sounded like prayer in the mother tongue. Barbara's breath caught, but she steadied herself and breathed out what she'd rehearsed while racing down the stairs from the attic.

"I didn't know they were cops. They passed through here but didn't stay long. They asked for directions. I believe they went down the alley and across King's Street."

"They weren't from around here and they aren't your regular customers. Of course they're cops!" Jerick yelled, veins showing on his temple. Barbara flinched, despite herself, the spittle that flew from his lips and the way he tightened his grip on the gun sent her mind reeling. Even if she threw herself onto the men, she couldn't protect her parents.

Should I give these strangers up? She thought, her eyes darted from one scowl to one firearm to the other.

"Look," Cory said, "you've done good business here for years. Cain likes you, you know that. But these guys, there more important than the money you bring in."

"What did they say to you? What did they ask? Don't waste our time either. Talk up!" Jerrick said. Barbara's mother had drawn her feet up into the couch and was trembling behind Mr. Waldron who was still praying or chanting something.

Barbara shivered at Cain's name. The thought of his gaze wriggling up her body before choosing her from the lineup of women who worked with her made her stomach turn. Catching herself again, she withdrew her smile and presented the professional composure she reserved for Cain.

"They didn't say anything to me and none of the girls attended to them. It's pretty early in the day guys."

Jerrick lowered his gun a little.

"They came in quietly and left quickly, then they went down the alley like I said."

"We'll see," Cory muttered, leaning to one side to peer at her parents and then glaring back at her.

"We'll see," He repeated. They turned and left. The door slammed with such force that Barbara's ankles threatened to buckle. Muddy boot prints imprinted into the edge of the plush faux fur carpet a few feet from where her parents sat, heads bowed, lips pressed tightly together. Mrs. Waldron was whimpering. Barbara's dad rubbed his wife's back gently; they rose after a while and shuffled to their bedroom. Barbara stood in the hallway between the attic stairs and the hallway where Cain's men had just stood. Her knees teetered on collapse and her stomach clenched so hard that by the time she realised she needed to breathe her abdomen hurt from the release.

After checking that her parents were okay—as far as that was possible, considering what just occurred—she waited ten minutes, changed into the oversized jersey and pajamas that had been lying on her bed, then ran up the attic stairs

"Are they gone?" said a voice from behind the stacks of fabric. Barbara stood in the doorway of the attic, still trembling. She had not turned the attic lights on; the fading sunlight of dusk cast an army of shadows throughout the room.

"Yes," Barbara said, her voice a cracking whisper. Her lips were as dry as the wind howling at the attic window, causing her to glance at it nervously in-between straining her ears to hear if Jerick and Cory had returned.

"What did you tell them about us?" said the short, middle-aged man who was still peeling away strips of fabric and thread from his head and shoulders as he emerged from the piles she had hid him and his partner under. The other man remained mostly hidden, his face peering out from between folds of cotton and satin and fleece.

"I heard the door slam, are they gone to get reinforcements?" the hidden man asked, his voice muddled by all the cloth.

"They brought the reinforcements with them, those guns were plenty," Barbara said. The man under the fabric shuddered so that folds of cloth slid from his head.

"They left," she said, repressing her own shivers.

"I told them you were headed through the alley and down King's Street."

"You covered for us?" the younger man said, finally emerging from his cloth cocoon. He was very average looking, nothing distinguishable about his face or frame. But Barbara's shoulders loosened, and her chest deflated when she looked into his eyes. They both wore all black, nondescript clothes with no cologne. She hadn't seen men this plainly dressed in so long that she tilted her head as she took them in. These two were the first men in a long time who hadn't spoken at her chest with greedy eyes. The younger man met and held her gaze, his smile soft. His posture relaxed but alert.

"I know why you're here."

Barbara's shoulders again tensed as she recalled the stories.

"Oh?" the older man said. His back was to her as he peered out the window. The younger man slumped into the only chair in the room, running fabric through his fingers, now looking everywhere but at her.

"Yes. You're special forces men. Some bigshots from the east funds your operations."

"What makes you say that?" the younger man said, his tone as flat as his partner's.

"I've heard about your group, you've been going across the province," she said, her voice dropping to an almost inaudible whisper.

"Wiping out gangs, drug lords, and sex trafficking rings," she finished.

"Interesting, what do you know about that? And why would men from that group come here?" the older man said. Barbara rolled her eyes and leaned against the door; fatigue had started to claim the use of her legs. He looked closer to her dad's age, maybe late forties, while the other fellow looked like he was her age or a bit older.

"Look, these guys might come back so let's skip the games. I know who you are. I know who funds you. I know you've never had an operation go bad. You've taken down everyone you've gone after. Ayden Farm Group is a big deal. The guy who owns it pretty much runs everything. If he wants it done, it's happening," she said flatly. The older man turned and faced her, his expression remained unchanged. She felt neither the need to run or to remove her clothes with these men.

"What do you want?" he asked. Barbara raised an eyebrow. Taking a deep breath, she threw out her request. If it failed, she had the savings to leave town if there was enough time before these guys raided and took down Cain.

"I want a way out for my family and me," she said.

"Done," he said, turning back to the window. Barbara's mouth fell open.

"What? Just like that?"

"As long as we leave here safe and you don't go back to Cain with any information, yes, why not? If you don't wanna live this life, we'll gladly help you stop."

He turned to face her again, making a few silent strides across the room. His unwavering gaze caught the glint of sunlight in the room. Barbara felt tears coming.

No. Not yet.

"Okay," she said. "How do I know you won't lock us all up or kill us when you do your raid?"

"Tie this red cloth on a window downstairs. We'll mark the spot and come and get you," the younger man said, standing.

"If it's not there when we come through and if the people you want to save aren't in the building, then that's on you," the older man said. Barbara nodded.

"Okay, will do," the said, sighing. She took a deep breath and passed him on her way to the window.

"Now, if you climb out this window and head across the parking lot and up the hill, you can lay low there until Jerick and Cory get back here. They'll probably send more people to search, and they'll likely have dogs to sniff you out. So don't leave the hill for a day or two if you can. They won't check there because there's no path to go up. And it's steep," she said, first pointing to an empty parking lot, then to a rocky hill in the distance.

"Alright. Thank you. The name's Salmon, what's yours?"

The older man extended his hand; Barbara shook it and nodded. The tears brimmed in the corners of her eyes.

"Barbara Waldron. Thank you! Thanks so much. Please don't forget us."

"You risked your lives for us. This is nothing. Rest easy," Salmon said. They waited for the sun to dip below the horizon before slipping through the window, climbing down into the alleyway and picking their way across the parking lot. Barbara watched them deftly cross the flat terrain and then just as easily work their way up the incline and over the crest. From the attic, she couldn't see the direction Jerrick and Cory had gone in but took solace in the fact that no lights or shouts rippled across the parking and in the direction where Salmon and his younger friend had gone. When she finally retreated to bed, it was as if she was the one who had climbed down the wall and up the hill. Sleep rescued her from her fatigue and delivered her into the hands of nightmares of Cain using a leather belt buckle to whip across her back while her parents were forced to watch from the couch.

Barbara clawed and groaned her way out of both her bedsheets and one final nightmare. Sitting up, she caught herself before she slipped from the king-sized bed that she was ready to forget. Sweat made her long hair cling to her face and neck, her fitted sheet had pulled away from the mattress in one corner and was bundled up around her along with the other sheet and the weighted comforter that usually helped her eke out some sleep. The bonnet she'd stuffed her hair into before bed was missing, likely trapped in the folds of sheets that were still wrapped around Barbara's legs. After reaching across to the nightstand to grab a scrunchie, she pushed the hair from her face and unpeeled herself from the sheets.

As she straightened the bedsheets, memories unfolded and hit her in the face like heat from fresh laundry. In one corner of the room sat a chest of drawers full of sheets that she'd assigned to repeat clients, as well as the ones she used for herself after each day's activities. Involuntarily, she rubbed her nose to rid it of the tingling recollection of the smoke that had clung to her body for three days after she'd burned the sheets that had been reserved for Cain. She shuddered, the sight of blood running out under ice cold water and baking soda permanently etched in her mind's eye. The echo of bruises and cuts from Cain's methods rippled through her body and made her nauseous. She clambered back into bed and squeezed her eyes shut. Against the black of her eyelids, images staggered and whimpered. Images of the younger women coming upstairs to get ice and stitches from Barbara's mother after being with Cain and his men. The stench of alcohol that trailed the dishevelled girls into the medical room her mother had set up was still gag-inducing to Barbara.

Mrs. Waldron would sit there, stitching cuts above the eyes and on the lips, while the girls put ice on bruised wrists and black and blue necklines. When she was done stitching, Mrs. Waldron deftly applied makeup to the bruises and the girls went back to work, tears perched on eyelids that were being paid to act. Moments later, plastic smiles and empty laughter would flow like the liquor being poured by Mr. Waldron at the minibar in the waiting area downstairs.

As reels of history played before her, Barbara lay flat on her back, with no pillow below her head, in the centre of the bed. The last time she'd used a pillow; Cain had held it over her face 'just because it was there.' The only way that man found stimulation was through inflicting pain. Barbara had found that out at fifteen when her mother introduced them to each other. He hadn't been 'King Cain' back then, and he hadn't needed to abuse alcohol or her body as much to get what he wanted.

Her mother had simply said, "he's doing really well for himself. He moves a lot of product. One day this city will be his. You might as well be his too." Initially—because Cain was attractive, and because it didn't hurt that much to be with him—Barbara had convinced herself she was having fun. The clothes, money, parties and access had thrilled her. But, before she knew it, she oversaw a whole house of women. Before she knew it, she was 'getting old', according to Cain and couldn't 'get him there' fast enough.

"Your mom retired for the same reason. This is a young woman's trade," Cain had said the day before he nearly suffocated her to get what he wanted from her body. After that, he'd turned to her sister and the younger ladies. Barbara had burned his sheets in the small backyard of the condo the next day, using it as kindling for a bonfire. He had sat around that fire with Jerrick, Cory and the other men, drinking, cackling like hyenas and tossing the newer girls around. For a fleeting moment, as the acrid smoke plumed upwards, Barbara had imagined he was wrapped up in the burning fabric. Now, the empire he'd built on selling women and white powder was about to be reduced to ash by someone else.

Let it all burn. You've earned it.

The entire complex of condos could see them surrounding the area. Armoured trucks with roof mounted machine guns were perched on hills, blocking roads and peeking out from bushes. In six hours, they rolled into position, gradually encircling the building until there were trucks on every side. Each unmarked, un-tinted truck housed at least four men in the same simple, black clothes that Salmon and the other young man had worn. The occupants sat in the vehicles, seemingly at ease. Barbara's sister was sure one of the guys was on his phone. Meanwhile, her neighbours were chattering so loudly, their voices pulsed through the walls.

There were no clients downstairs either. The girls had taken to the bar and from the sounds of it, they were all deep in the bottles. The sounds of breaking glass and furniture falling over mixed in with raucous cackling and the occasional scream. In the streets below, Cain's men trotted to-and-fro, as fast as they could move with their semiautomatic weapons. Nervous energy vibrated through the air like echoes in an empty room.

Barbara's chest had gone from constricted to drumming frantically to now a dull ache.

"Is this how they always operate?" her father asked, peering out the window for the umpteenth time, fiddling with the red cord to make sure it was visible from a distance.

"Actually, no," Barbara said, her words dry and raspy. She stepped past her preteen cousins and aunt who were playing a board game at the dining table. Beside her mom, her uncle was reading something on a tablet.

"They do something different every time. Cain was prepared for the drones and helicopters they used out in Misruton to take down that cult," she said, raising her voice above the crescendoing background noise.

"The one with the human trafficking and sacrificing their sons?" Mrs. Waldron asked.

"Yup," Barbara said. She continued pacing as her dad peered out the window again. Her mom was doing macramé, swearing under her breath on account of the mistakes her trembling hands were leaving in her knots. Tapping her knee against the table leg, Barbara's sister scrolled through social media while glancing up at the window at every new sound.

The special ops men had been cold silent except for the faint rumbling of their vehicles. After realising that they couldn't find Salmon and his companion, Jerrick and Cory had run back to Cain. He'd in turn tried to escape into the adjacent city where he had—according to rumour—safehouses and more men working for him. The girl who had been at his penthouse had been sent back to Barbara early. According to her, Cain hadn't made it very far on account of the armoured trucks that had already pulled up ahead of the others. Angry and out of options, Cain had stationed men, hidden on almost every roof with every gun in the condo complex, aiming at the trucks.

"They won't shoot though. Cowards," Barbara said under her breath. Her sister immediately glanced in her direction; Barbara shook her head and kept pacing. Her sister was still looking at her, frowning and pouting. Barbara's plush slippers created static against the carpet every now and then. Her sister sighed and went back to scrolling, her pout still evident even with her head bowed.

"Those guys are the real deal," Mr. Waldron said, pointing with his lips at the vehicles.

"They shut down Misruton slowly and painfully. Then they killed all the dudes who came after them to get the slaves back. They didn't take prisoners." He added. Mrs. Waldron swore again, she'd missed another knot. Mr.

Waldron's hushed tones sat like a weighted blanket in the room. Barbara shuddered, stopped near the window beside him and peeked over his shoulder.

"Are we sure they'll keep their word?" She asked. Her words made her shiver again. Cain was definitely going to get taken down. She didn't want to get taken down with him.

"Maybe we should find a way out? They might kill everyone." Her mom said, her voice barely making it across the living room.

Barbara looked at the suitcases they had packed and the rest of the family silently looking to her. Faces she'd watched grow and age, faces she'd held as babies, people who'd relied on her business to eat and have a roof.

How am I still the one in charge? She thought, sighing. Her shoulders sagged and her heart resumed its treadmill run. A decade ago, when she started hosting girls and catering to more than just Cain's needs, she'd stopped being invited to family events and people had stopped picking up her calls. Now many of those same people lived in the complex and were sitting right in front of her, patrons of funds she'd earned from those same clients.

Funny how a recession can bring people together.

Sighing, Barbara straightened her back one more time.

"There's nowhere to go. Plus, there's no way out of the complex. Our only hope is that these men will take care of us." Grumbled agreement spluttered up across the living room and then suddenly died down. Someone was using a loudspeaker somewhere outside.

Barbara tiptoed and looked over her dad's shoulder again. Bodies pressed into hers as more family members tried to see as well. The red cord outside the window was still firmly tied and waving in the light breeze.

"...and we can end this peacefully. There does not need to be any bloodshed."

The words vibrated in Barbara's ears causing her to tremble.

"Cain's not gonna go for that," her cousin muttered. Barbara could tell from the voice that it was the cousin that people called her younger twin. She was right, Cain would think he could fight his way out like he'd fought for everything else.

Barbara's father stiffened and then dragged her and the others below the windowsill and covered their heads. The faint sounds of whizzing bullets colliding with nearby walls created a backdrop to the blood curdling screams of her neighbours and the wails of men falling from roofs and windows. Eventually, the screams subsided and the only sounds to be heard were those of walls being devoured by artillery. A marching-band drumbeat of bullets raged at the complex. Her ears ached and her breaths came ragged as though she'd been running. Behind her, her mom was crouched beside the sofa, mumbling prayers. Barbara's sister had ducked under the table and was visibly trembling. The children were all on their stomachs, heads held down by Barbara's aunt.

As the hailstorm of ammo pelted almost everything, Barbara's window remained intact. Crouched against the wall, cradled by her dad, she waited, praying for the first time since kindergarten that somehow, they'd make it out alive.

Moments later there came a bone-chilling silence. Still, no one dared move. Barbara scanned the room, everyone was intact. There was no blood in the room. She gritted her teeth and shook away the memories of being in the bathroom stemming her own bleeding while Cain lay on her bed, filling her room with cigar smoke.

There was a knock at her door. A gentle, firm knock.

"It's Salmon. If you're in there, it's safe now. Let's go."

"Oh, thank God," her mom and aunt said simultaneously.

Barbara looked at her mom, pale as the walls, crouched against the corner of the chaise. Pulling on the windowsill, Barbara stood, walked unsteadily towards the door and checked the peephole to be sure.

"Thank God."

Naomi

Naomi's tears flowed like wine at a wedding. Bitterness filled the back of her throat as she formed a crumpled smile. Ruth's grip as they hugged was firm, certain. Naomi wept into her daughter-in-law's neck on the porch of the house that had stopped being her home the moment her beloved Eli had died.

Two years, eight months and four days ago, she'd had to watch her sons Mahlon and Kleon as pallbearers walking with her beloved's body and placing him into the ground. Orpah–Kleon's wife–and Ruth had each held one of her arms during the burial procession to stop her from fainting. Had it not been for Ruth keeping a firm arm around Naomi's waist, she might have flung herself into the casket while the minister was saying final rights. None of Eli's kin would ever see him again. She couldn't even afford to send his body home.

For months after his funeral, she'd close her eyes and smell the hospital cleaning solution and see his sunken face and neck not moving and feel his fingers go lifeless in her palm. His life insurance and the combination of both their pensions had paid off the house and given Naomi enough to live on each month. But she'd stopped living the moment Eli's lifeline cut out in that hospital room.

The lonely echoes of her footsteps and how loud the microwave was without Eli in the house had driven Naomi to confining herself to her room until hunger or a need to use the bathroom drove her from under her bedsheets. Kleon and

Mahlon had each taken turns stopping by the house once or twice a week after Eli had passed. From the time he'd gotten ill to less than three months later when he stopped squeezing her hand in that hospital room, she'd lost as much weight as he had. Mahlon would come by and heave her out of the bed and plop her down at the dinner table and stand over her until she finished the meal Ruth had made. Kleon would carry her outside in his arms like Eli had carried her into their home on the evening of their wedding day. If not for her boys, she'd have let herself join Eli where he was. Pangs of unreachable ache in her chest snagged her breath every time she passed a portrait of the family in the living room. She'd considered taking them all down but could barely bring herself to look at them, much more to remove them. After getting lost staring at the background in one of the pictures taken when her sons were still little boys back in the old country, she'd started thinking about going home.

Ruth and Naomi were both sitting on the front porch on the outdoor sofa that had been Eli's favourite place to read the news and reminisce about their childhood town. Naomi had not been on that porch since right after the last funeral. With Ruth in the house, she refused to leave her room, and Ruth couldn't scoop her up the way Mahlon or Kleon would. She was only outside because the real estate agent had just stopped by to give them the news. A lock of Naomi's ash grey hair waved across her wrinkled cheeks. Frowning, she snatched it from her face and tucked it behind her hair. Ruth's recently cut red hair shimmered in the light breeze.

In front of the house, the well-kept lawn sat in contrast to the small flower garden that had become overgrown with weeds. Naomi hadn't touched it in almost two years. Stuck in the lawn was a for sale sign with the word 'sold' taped over it. The house had only been on the market for a few months. Naomi's last ties to these suburbs and this country had been signed away to some young couple who still had their whole lives ahead of them.

"Are you sure?" Naomi said between sobs into the soft fabric of Ruth's blouse.

"You're stuck with me," Ruth whispered.

"You might as well be my birth mom at this point. There's nothing left for me here. If you're going, then so am I." Ruth's words reverberated through Naomi.

Moments later, Naomi pulled away from Ruth's embrace to lean back into the sofa and press her hands into her temple.

First El, now the boys. My boys. Naomi thought amidst the headache that had been plaguing her since the funerals. Less than five months ago, she'd watched six men she did not know carry both of her young sons through the same public plot where they'd laid Eli. There had been no family. It hadn't been her church. The men in her life were now surrounded by strangers, and she was a stranger to this country that she had never liked in the first place. The recession that had lured her and Eli from home with the promise of great jobs and a fresh start had gotten stale faster than fish under the sun. Eventually, they landed the jobs and bought the house. The boys went off to college, got their own jobs and found wives. Then the epidemic found them. First it drained Eli of his bright eyes and sweet smile. Less than three years later, it snatched Mahlon and stole Kleon shortly afterwards. So many had died that it stopped airing as breaking news. It had broken Naomi repeatedly to first watch her husband and then both her sons get ill and die to a sickness with no cure and barely any treatment. Her boys hadn't even hit thirty yet.

"There's nothing left for me here." She'd said to Ruth and Orpah a month after Kleon's funeral. When both young ladies had offered to move back to the old country with Naomi, she'd spent days trying to dissuade them both. Orpah hadn't been hard to convince. Ruth, on the other hand, had already moved in with Naomi after Mahlon had been hit by the virus. Orpah held a good job in the city and was still quite close to her family. Ruth had been the one to follow Naomi to sabbath services and ask her about her home country and learn how to cook all the meals. Ruth had been invested, getting close to Naomi from before she'd married Mahlon.

Naomi frowned as she looked across at Ruth who was typing a resignation letter on her phone, while humming one of Naomi's favourite songs. Naomi glanced up and silently groaned at the neighbours' children cycling around the block once again. Ruth and Mahlon had tried to get pregnant with no luck before Mahlon fell ill. Orpah and Kleon had been trying too but between Eli passing and careers and then the epidemic, nothing had happened.

Probably for the best. How would the girls have managed? The familiar pang shook Naomi's chest, prompting her to rise and head inside to make them both some tea. Her eyes watered again at the thought of having company both on the plane and back home when she landed. She'd never liked traveling alone, living alone even less so.

"Thank you, Ruth," she whispered, leaning on the counter. With the recession over, things back home were better than they'd known them to be growing up. Naomi sucked her teeth, frowning at the thought that Eli never got to see his home or his business flourish once more.

"I won't die here. I can't," she murmured, fighting back another deluge of tears. The family plot back home would be hard to visit; the family had likely put a placeholder tombstone there for El and the boys. Blinking away wetness, she stirred the tea and covered the sugar canister. She needed to book a flight with two tickets, as soon as she confirmed with Ruth when she wanted to leave.

Waves of the smell of bread and olive oil and wine bathed Naomi's senses. The strong wind kicked up dust and memories, making her eyes water behind her glasses. She lifted her glasses and wiped her eyes with the back of her hand and sniffled.

"Are you okay, Miss Naomi?" Ruth asked, stopping with the two suitcases to peer around at Naomi's face.

"I'm fine, I'm fine. I'm just old and the place is dusty," Naomi said, waving her on. Ruth chuckled and kicked out the suitcases to a rolling position. Naomi straightened her glasses and kept walking. The shop signs and paint on the walls were paler than she remembered. The people working in the shops were photocopies of the people she'd gone to school and ran the fields with. They'd been children when she left, close in age to Mahlon and Kleon. They were alive and smiling as they served the throngs of tourists. Small children zipped in and around the shops too. Naomi swallowed her tears. There were so many tourists that she was being jostled every few steps. There had never been this many before the recession.

"Hey Ruth, over there, that's where the boys went to high school," Naomi said, pointing to a building that wore its age in weathered red brick with myriad small cracks running through it.

"Oh, wow. I see how near it is to the shops, but I still don't get why they went home for lunch every day, even in high school," Ruth said, shading her eyes so she could look over at the school.

"You've tasted my cooking," Naomi said, a wry smile forming. Ruth chuckled and nodded.

"Fair enough," Ruth said. Tourists slipped in and out of their line of sight in broad hats and big sunglasses, sipping wine that was either older than Ruth or freshly pressed. The tang of wine in the air was accompanied by the memory of the boys eating grapes until their tongues were stained and their appetites were ruined.

"Well, it's more that this community is old and old-fashioned and we didn't have a place to really eat lunch there. Most kids would run home for lunch or to their parents' shops," Naomi said, staining under the weight of nostalgia.

"Nowhere to eat?" Ruth said, her mouth slightly agape.

"School is for learning. That was the motto. Plus, there isn't much space. Too many tourists. Schools aren't an attraction," Naomi said, she sighed and kept pulling the two carry-on suitcases that she'd had to fight Ruth to carry. Ruth had fully intended to carry them all somehow. Even after Naomi had told her that to get through the heart of the town, you had to walk or ride a bicycle because cars weren't allowed on the old stone roads.

As they passed shops, various sights and the major wineries, Naomi pointed out most of the ones that Mahlon and Kleon had frequented, as well as all the people they were related to.

"So many cousins," Ruth said. "Your family is huge."

Naomi shrugged.

"The nights are cold, and cellphones weren't around back then. People needed something to do."

"Making babies was a hobby?" Ruth asked, lowering her tone so that the tourists couldn't hear her.

"Well... not that part," Naomi said, blushing. Ruth burst out laughing but quickly bit her lips after the stares she was drawing. Many of the tourists and vendors turned, saw two people with suitcases and went right back to whatever they were doing.

Three hours later, they made it to the family home where another cousin had been house sitting. Naomi's ankles hurt from all the standing around and talking that had stopped them getting here sooner. One by one the cousins had realised she was back and had come to ask entirely too many questions.

"Where're the boys and Eli?"

"Who's this young lady?"

"How come you're just coming back?"

"It's good to see you, you've lost so much weight though, I'm trying to lose weight but it's just not happening for me."

The questions had tumbled over her patience like freshly picked grapes but nowhere as sweet.

Naomi rolled her suitcases into the living room, hugged her cousin, gave her a 'we've talked on the phone, don't ask me anything' look and fell back into the nearest seat. After closing her eyes and leaning back, she realised it was the armchair where Eli would read the paper and drink his tea. Across from her, on the mantle were pictures she'd long forgotten about. Scrunching up her face, she squeezed her eyes shut against the tears. Naomi heaved a sigh and tussled with the urge to remove herself from Eli's chair. Ruth was still touring the house with Naomi's cousin who was loudly giving her history that fuelled the tears brimming beneath closed eyes.

"Bye Auntie Nay! I'm glad you're back home. We missed you. I'll see you on Sabbath. Pastor is looking forward to seeing you and meeting Ruth." Naomi's cousin said as she stepped through the door.

"Goodbye dear. Tell your mother hello for me. I didn't see her in town," Naomi responded, still slumped in Eli's armchair.

"She's still on shift at the winery."

Naomi waved goodbye and Ruth closed the front door behind the young lady.

"I'm really excited to go to church here with you!" Ruth said, her face was aglow. She'd been staring and smiling the whole walk up to the house. Even during the repeated conversations, she'd smiled and nodded and answered the same questions repeatedly. The amount of people who had asked her about her home country and their ways of doing things was bordering on absurd.

"Who asks a stranger that many questions? You'd think they'd learn how annoying it is from the tourists," Naomi muttered. She winced at the memory of the questions about Eli, Mahlon and Kleon that Ruth had gracefully answered a dozen times.

"They got sick in the epidemic and passed away. It affected more males than females." Ruth had said. The whole time she'd repeated it for new enquirers; she kept a straight face and even tone. Naomi had bit her lips and eked out a whisper of a smile for the most part. The image of Eli's jaunt frame in the last few weeks contrasted too heavily with the pictures on the mantle of him among the grape vines carrying baskets larger than his torso. Naomi's chest tightened.

"I don't think I'm going to church this sabbath. I'm tired," Naomi said.

Ruth frowned at this comment, opened her mouth to say something and then closed it, walked over and sat down right where Mahlon had loved to sit. Naomi rubbed the arm of the sofa gently, smiling.

"I miss them too, I can't imagine how hard all this is for you. I'm sorry," Ruth said softly.

"I think I'll go to bed early tonight," Naomi said, ignoring the growing pang in her chest. Ruth's frown deepened, then she smiled.

"It really was a long flight, and it took so long to walk up here. Some rest would do us both good. I'll sit here for a bit and then turn in as well," Ruth said.

Naomi groaned as she rose from the armchair, her wrists trembled. Eli had always said the chair was only comfortable until it was time to get up, after that it was a fight. A faint smile visited her lips briefly as she remembered his little shimmy to the edge of the chair before quickly launching himself forward with his knees. Freeing her wrists, she let herself fall back. Ruth gasped. Naomi lifted an assuring palm; Ruth relaxed her shoulders and unclenched her jaw.

"I'm just old, not glass. This is how Eli would get out of this chair," she said, demonstrating the shimmy and shove that launched her forward. Ruth started giggling, her mouth covered, then burst out laughing and fell over into the sofa. Naomi couldn't help the smile that forced its way out alongside the tears that now flowed by her cheeks.

The joy of the Lord. I'm glad one of us has it. She thought, picking up the central photo from the mantle.

"If I hear another stupid question, I'm going to be rude to someone," Naomi muttered.

Ruth stopped laughing and made her way over to the mantle. As they looked at each picture together, Naomi whispered the stories around them all. Eventually, she set the last frame down and rested her head lightly on the smooth wooden mantle, the smell of the old timber replaced by years of furniture polish. A deluge of slow images danced across her closed eyelids:

Eli yelling at the boys to go play outside so that she could clean.

Him kissing the back of her neck while she wiped dust from the mantle.

Her sipping a cool drink he'd made for her.

Five-year-old Mahlon asking about a picture of his grandparents for the umpteenth time.

The pang in her ribcage was loud. Her knees whispered threats, she started shuffling towards the door to the hallway that would take her to the bedrooms at the back of the house.

"I pray you have sweet sleep, Miss Nay."

"Thanks, Ruru. Thank you."

***

"No, I'm not using that name any longer. Please use my maiden name, thank you," Naomi said. Her words falling like icicles.

"Ma'am?" The young bank teller said. Naomi kept her gaze on the document before her.

"Please refer to me by my maiden name. Is there anything else I need to sign?"

"Yes, uh, sorry, no ma'am. Your retirement funds will come to this account starting next month. Since you've already closed the accounts you had with the other bank, this is your primary account once more. Thank you for banking with us. Is there anything else I can help you with?" He said after straightening his tie nervously. His face had once been the face of an old friend of Eli's. He'd passed away too.

At least he's buried here, and your mother can still look at you to see him. Naomi thought. She shook the thought loose and looked back down at the new debit card and accompanying documents.

"Yes, please remind me what the account balance is."

Seven minutes later, Naomi stepped squinting into the sunlight and the sweetness of grapes in the air.

I'll have to sell the shop building. She thought, biting her lips to prevent herself from pouting. She had passed Eli's old shop on her way to the bank and had forcibly held her head straight to avoid seeing the still legible sign that Eli had hand-painted when she was pregnant with Mahlon and repainted with the boys when they were both old enough to help him. The title of the business was still in her and Eli's names, and the building was still there, being rented out as storage by a few other shops around it. Shielding her face from the glare off the cut stone street, she stepped out toward the family home. As she neared Eli's shop, a young man stepped out into the busy street and signalled her over. At first, she wasn't sure he was calling her until he called her by her married name. Grimacing, she weaved through the crowd and made her way over to him.

"Glad to have you back Mrs. Dav..." Jacob Simons the third said, Naomi held her hand up and the young shop owner bit his lips.

"Please refer to me as Miss Naomi or use my maiden name. I'm no longer Mrs. anything."

"My apologies Miss Naomi, I was saying that I appreciate you letting us use the space for such a low fee. Sorry I can't buy it off you."

The shop now run by Jacob—he had taken over from his grandfather—was left-adjacent Eli's shop. The other two shopkeepers using the space noticed she was talking to Jacob and added themselves to the conversation as soon as they were done with the customers before them. After similar greetings, the young people–now running shops that their parents had retired from–shared a similar sentiment to Jacob. They didn't do enough business to use that much more space. Twenty minutes of small talk later, Naomi excused herself, citing her age, and continued down the street.

A young lady who had been singing last sabbath passed Naomi going the opposite direction and waved sheepishly. Naomi nodded and held her head straight. Sabbath service had been surprisingly refreshing. The acapella youth choir had hit some notes that still hummed through her muscles four days later. As much as she'd wanted to avoid it, the hugs and welcomes she'd received had lulled the pain in her chest to a mere whisper. Every time it flared up, she thought back to a warm embrace or a beaming smile.

And the way they'd received Ruth had been enough to drive her to tears. Ruth's name was already on the list to join the choir and the new members' classes. She'd ended up coming home late after Sabbath, out having a meal with the other young women. Naomi scowled, she had declined all invitations, especially from the people who pretended they didn't hear when she asked to be called by her maiden name.

After service, pastor Levy had vehemently refused to call her by her maiden name when he came over to welcome her back.

The audacity, pastor or not, I'm many years his senior. I went to school with his parents.

"Respectfully Sister, I cannot agree to call you by a name you no longer wear. Unless you remarry, I see no reason you should discard your late husband's name," he'd said, his face holding a pleasant and annoyingly genuine smile.

"What does he know?" Naomi mumbled. Rolling her eyes, she stepped into a newer shop—it hadn't been there before the recession—to browse and pick up a few things for the house. She weaved through the aisles of the haphazardly organised store.

"He's barely forty-five. All I'm doing is removing the joy from my name the way God removed the joy from my life. Why should I hold on to anything beautiful?"

A familiar looking young man peered curiously at Naomi as she murmured to herself. Keeping her eyes trained on the items stocked on the shelves, she kept walking until the young man shrugged and went back to his own browsing. The store was oddly reminiscent of Ruth's country, Naomi's chest tightened. Every few steps she took, she was met with items she used to buy for the boys or Eli to try. She even saw a brand of drink that Mahlon had been obsessed with for over a year. Smiling weakly at the attendant, she dipped out of the store and headed straight home and into bed.

***

"Miss Nay, I've been looking at what I can get into around town, and I think I'll go volunteer at the park," Ruth said, she was pacing in the hallway next to the office where Naomi was working.

"They have high tourist traffic and lots of rides and stalls that need help. Maybe they'll offer me a job."

"That's an excellent idea Ruth, dear. I pray they give you a chance. They'll see your hard work, I just know it," Naomi said, looking up at Ruth and smiling. The day after Mahlon's funeral, Ruth had cleaned the apartment they'd shared, packed everything she owned, sorted Mahlon's things and moved in with Naomi. The girl couldn't sit idly, she didn't know how. She didn't know how to rest either. When Naomi had told her that the word sabbath actually meant rest, she had been visibly appalled. Naomi had laughed so hard her sides had hurt.

What was hurting now was Naomi's head and it was barely seven thirty in the morning. Years of files spread before her, littered with fine print that strained her eyes. Again, she pushed her glasses up the bridge of her nose and pulled a document closer to her face.

El, I don't know how you did this for so many years. She thought as Ruth disappeared to get ready to leave for the park. Being away for almost twenty years, leaving behind a floundering business had generated a lot of paperwork. Naomi had always preferred working at the vineyard or in the shop itself over ploughing through paper. When they had moved to the new country, she'd taken a job at an Ayden agro-processing site to avoid the secretarial position Eli jokingly taunted her with.

Later that day, Ruth's return was a welcome reprieve from the lake of papers spread across Eli's old office desk and the tables Naomi had hauled into the office to give herself more room to work.

"Mr. Bo was very kind to me, shook my hand and offered me a job and even paid me for today." Ruth said as soon as she closed the front door behind her. Her jeans were stained and her hair—frizzy and damp—was caught up in one of Naomi's old handkerchiefs.

"Oh? Bo is running the park now? That makes sense, his family has run it for years. He's El's younger cousin, you know. El babysat him and his siblings quite often," Naomi said, her mind drifting to dinners at Bo's parents' house that she'd attended as a newlywed.

"Oh yes! He told me. He told me a few stories before I got back to work. He seems very nice," Ruth said, the giddy energy she was giving off made Naomi smile.

"Definitely stay there. That was a good choice dear. He'll treat you well," Naomi said, nodding. Eli had always spoken well of Aunt Barbara, Bo's mom. He had snuck over to their house often to eat the meals she offered. Eli had always enjoyed foreign food. Aunt Barbara had moved to the country as a young woman and brought some of her culture with her.

It wasn't surprising that Bo was as kind as his mom had been before she passed away.

Ruth was humming and smiling so much for the next few weeks that it started to rub off on Naomi. She was in the office again; she'd had to wipe down every surface and the floors to stop herself and Ruth sneezing every time they ventured in there. It had taken a few hours to get it clean enough. Still, every time she went in there, her nose tingled from dust in the air and hidden in places she hadn't reached. Throwing open the single window helped a bit but the urge to whip out a hundred wet wipes was still strong as she wiped her nose and straightened the papers.

"I think I ought to sell it. Thankfully, El left everything in good standing. He never did like owing anyone." She said, placing the sorted documents into folders and binders.

The recession had been devastating but not sudden. Three seasons in a row, the vignerons and their teams struggled to squeeze substandard yields from their fields. More and more tours were cancelled until the streets were all but devoid of tourists. The park and many of the shops closed shortly afterwards. That was when people started leaving. Head-hunters from factory jobs put up posters and handed out business cards. Naomi had been prepared to grit her teeth and bare it.

It was never supposed to have lasted so long, she thought.

Then the wineries sold through reserve stock and aged collections and more stores closed. Folks left their homes with family and migrated as soon as they could book flights. Early on, Eli had sold everything in the store at discounted prices and paid off everyone they'd owed. They'd even tucked away a bit of savings. Frowning, she remembered Eli convincing her that moving abroad for a few years would work out for them.

"Without tourists coming through, we'll run out of money in a year. I can find a factory job and so can you. At least until the boys are older, then maybe we can save more and move back here."

I'm back, El. But you're not with me. That evil place killed you and my boys. Why did you leave me like this? Why did God have to take you from me so soon?

***

A brilliant kaleidoscope of sunset colours spreading around the hill across from the back porch heralded the coming end of the summer tourist season. Ruth had worked with Bo's team the entire time, making a steady income. Naomi sighed and smiled. Ruth had handed Naomi more than half her pay every week to put towards household expenses. The money that the young woman did keep was split between personal bills, savings and tithing. Naomi remembered her early years sewing and baking into the night and the joy of placing an envelope with her tithe in the basket on sabbath. She'd met Eli because of tithing. He'd been working as an usher, passing the basket along the aisles of the pews. One sabbath, he handed her the basket and a handwritten note asking her on a date. His penmanship had been so bad that she waited after service to ask him what the note said.

"I guess it doesn't matter what I actually wrote," he joked as he walked her home that evening.

"I would like to take you out for dinner," Eli said. Naomi blushed, pushing black hair from her face. "I don't eat at that restaurant, and you don't have a car so we can't go to the city." Naomi said, thinking of the single restaurant in town. Eli looked at her, rubbing his chin.

"Besides," she continued, "my cooking is better than that place anyways."

"Well then," Eli said, grinning, "Tell me what ingredients to bring and I'll come over to your place and be your sous chef."

Naomi smiled with tears in her eyes as their first date played out in her mind. Eli had been so clumsy in the kitchen that Naomi's father had needed to rescue him by asking him for help in the backyard. Naomi and her mother had laughed so hard at the mess he'd made.

Naomi wiped tears from her face and made her way to the kitchen where she'd baked and cooked with Eli until he was making meals he'd invented for her. She'd fallen in love with his cooking after the first few years. His love for foreign food had led to him coming up with meal ideas to surprise her every time he shooed her out of the kitchen.

El, my sweet Eli. Naomi thought. She did the dishes and stared out the window at the backyard where Mahlon and Kleon had ruined sabbath and school clothes so often that she kept rolls of uniform fabric on hand to mend or replace them.

Naomi smiled. She hummed one of the songs from her childhood that she'd taught Ruth. The young lady was out visiting some older members of the community who couldn't leave their homes on their own anymore. The ache in her heart lessened as the weeks rolled on. She found herself smiling like this often. When she moved through the house and was reminded of Eli and the boys, the pain came out in teary smiles. And she hadn't minded as much when the nosy family members who stopped by the house lobbed questions at her about her experience in the other country. Showing pictures of the boys going off to university and their weddings didn't trigger panic attacks or a river of tears.

As the heat of summer blurred into temperatures that didn't burn the skin on contact, Naomi refurbished some tools from the old shed in the backyard. With Ruth's help and the help of some of the young men who had grown up with Mahlon and Kleon, they pulled down the old treehouse and broken-down swing set and cleaned up Naomi's overrun, unused garden. In the breezy evenings, accented by the taste of crushed grapes in the air, Naomi tilled the soil and transplanted seedlings of her favourite flowers and some of the vegetables Eli had loved preparing. Tiny rows of green waved at her from the patch of deep, rich brown topsoil, transplanting her to a time when Eli would bring her juice concoctions that made her shiver at their sweet tartness.

Ruth had only a few more days to go before the end of the season. Naomi wondered where her daughter-in-law would go next. The kind of work she'd done in her own country did not really exist in this small wine community.

"There has to be something that Bo will allow her to do in the off-season. She hasn't stopped talking about him and he hasn't stopped going out of his way to see her. Park owners don't arbitrarily walk around checking in on new staff," Naomi said to herself as she watered the seedlings. She smirked and whispered a similar prayer to what she'd said when Mahlon had first told her about Ruth.

"Lord, I'm not opposed to my daughter marrying this man, you know. He's a bit older than her but that never stopped anyone before."

She chuckled and made her way into the house. Ruth hadn't admitted it, but she spoke about Bo the way she had spoken about Mahlon. No one could replace Eli or the thirty-four and a half years they'd spent together, but there was no reason for Ruth to also stay a widow.

"Besides Lord, I want some grandchildren."

A few hours later, Naomi was slipping in and out of sleep in Eli's rocking chair on the front porch. The gate opened,

Naomi stirred. Ruth approached the house dragging her feet. The yawn and stretch that followed made Naomi chuckle.

"Child, you sound older than I. Why do your joints creak?" Naomi said.

"My generation isn't well built," Ruth said. She collapsed onto the outdoor sofa. Naomi smiled and shook her head.

"So, how was your day?"

"The admin stuff I've been getting into is very interesting. I just wish I had more time. Friday is so close," Ruth said between yawns. Naomi sat up and rubbed her chin. Administration wasn't far off from what Ruth had done in the other country.

"There's normally an end of season get-together held on the park grounds. You should dress up and go sit with Bo when the party is about to end. He's a nice, unmarried man." Naomi said. Ruth turned beet red and looked down, wringing her hands.

"'Get-together' sounds so old." Ruth said, her voice was hushed. A chorus of cicadas and birds signalled the beginning of dusk. Ruth's phone vibrated once.

"I am old." Naomi said, shrugging. "And I'm not calling it a party because it isn't one. There's no dancing and the music is just background noise while people eat and socialise."

"Definitely not a party. That's nothing like back home," Ruth said. Her head was still down; she stared at the notification icon against the darkened screen of her phone.

"I'm glad it's not, I hardly slept through a single Saturday night," Naomi said, remembering the board games she played with Eli until her eyes finally surrendered to sleep amidst the walls vibrating to raucous sounds that by all rights shouldn't be classified as music.

"Regardless, you should really put on a nice dress, some perfume and jewelry and make sure he sees you," Naomi said, settling back into Eli's chair and pulling her comforter up to her chin.

"Isn't that a little bit too forward?" Ruth said, her blush returning.

"Did I say sleep with him? Just present yourself. I'm sure he'll do the rest," Naomi said.

Ruth's reddening face and the small nod she did before jumping up and dashing into the house and up the stairs made Naomi burst out laughing. She shook her head and kept shaking it to avoid the thought of Mahlon and Kleon. Ruth still talked about them often, especially after getting off the phone with Orpah. Naomi glanced over at the place on the front lawn where the boys had stood for a picture in soiled school clothes, posing with their father. The dull ache slowly spread through her chest and triggered her tears. She pulled her legs into the rocking chair and allowed the memories to reel out before her.

I think I can miss the boys and still make sure Ruru has a good future. Naomi thought, leaning back in the chair and watching the last bit of orange and purple slip away into the dusk.

Two thirty-five am. Eli had died exactly three years ago. Naomi sat at the foot of the armchair in the living room, rocking back and forth. Her right hand clamped over her mouth and her left hugged her drawn up knees. She was still sobbing so hard that her chest was heaving and her shoulders trembled. Ruth was, thankfully, fast asleep in Mahlon's old room upstairs at the far end of the house.

The dream about Eli pulling his hand away and turning on his side as he lay in the hospital bed had become a nightly occurrence. In the dream, he died with his back to her. Sometimes, he'd pull his hand away, get up and start walking down a long hall. Mahlon and Kleon would then join him and no matter how she called after them, they did not turn around. She ran after them, only to fall on her face in a pool of hospital disinfectant. When she looked up, they were gone. She had woken up with her nightgown soaked in sweat and her throat bitter and dry.

As she'd done every night for the last week, she'd left her bedroom and headed for the armchair. It didn't smell like him anymore. He was not there to run his hands through her hair as she sat on a cushion between his legs and sewed something for one of the boys. He was still gone. The chair was still empty.

"I still miss you," she said to the empty chair. The pangs in her chest were thunder in her ear. Her breaths were short and clipped and every joint hurt. She glanced at the clock as she clambered into the armchair. Six minutes after three. Her knees felt like crushed grapes and her arms screamed agony when she used them to pull herself up.

"Maybe I'll die and catch up to you, El," she said as the pressure in her chest pounded its way through the rest of her body. Her thoughts fogged over as dizziness set in. She closed her eyes.

I want to catch up to you, El. Don't leave me again.

Panicked, Ruth tore through the house, yelling for Naomi the next morning. As was her custom, she'd stopped by Naomi's room for morning prayer, only to see an empty bed. Naomi never missed morning prayer. When she finally found Naomi in the armchair, Ruth had to check her pulse to confirm that she was breathing. Naomi was curled, in a fetal position, in the chair and her nightgown was damp with sweat.

"All your vitals are normal for your age. We'll see what the blood tests say when those come back but I don't see any signs of anything physically wrong with you," the town doctor said. She packed her bag, nodded at Ruth and left after answering a few questions out of earshot of Naomi. Naomi scowled at Ruth momentarily but did not have the energy to maintain it. Sipping the tea Ruth had brought her, she opted instead to glare at the young lady.

"Why did you call Mavis? I'm fine, I just fell asleep in the chair"

"I left you in your room last night," Ruth said, lines creasing her forehead. Her eyes were soft with held tears. Naomi sighed.

"Ruru, I am fine."

"Today is the day he passed.," Ruth whispered. "I can't eat or sleep most Mondays. Every week my phone feels like fire in my hand. I remember the call about Mahlon." Naomi's own tears spilled out and ran down her gaunt face. Ruth sniffled and rubbed her face dry.

"Mamma Nay," she said, kneeling before Naomi, "Sometimes the hurt is too much to carry inside. You're strong, but this weighs too much," Ruth said, Naomi met her daughter-in-law's gaze. She could barely see her through the tears and without her glasses.

"No one has time for my grief," Naomi said, Ruth took her hands into hers.

"I do."

"Save your I do for Bo," Naomi said. Ruth's eyes instantly overflowed with tears. Naomi winced.

"I know that losing them hurts you, especially papa El. I don't pretend to fully understand losing your whole family. But I am here. Even if something does happen with Bo. You're my family first."

Naomi groaned and pulled Ruth into a hug.

"Ruru, I'm sorry I said that. That was not appropriate," Naomi whispered in Ruth's ear. Ruth nodded and returned the embrace.

"This pain won't leave my chest," Naomi said. "Most days I can ignore it; some days it takes me captive."

"Mamma Nay," Ruth said, pulling away just enough to look into Naomi's eyes. "A therapist could help you, maybe. I don't think it's healthy to keep that all locked up in you. I thought you were gone when I saw you here this morning."

Naomi sighed and avoided Ruth's gaze.

"I'm too old for therapy."

***

She'd gone through half a ream of paper printing everything that had been on the computer.

"Darn screens everywhere, my poor old eyes," Naomi said to herself as she placed more files into each of the five piles that she had before her. Ruth was out with Bo again. Naomi had stopped counting how many coffees and dinner dates they'd had in the last few months. Naomi chuckled; Bo had asked Ruth to dinner almost the same way Eli had asked her. Ruth hadn't said what Naomi had though, there were more restaurants in town now and Bo had a car.

"El made walking and taking taxis fun though. My sweet adventurer," Naomi said. Her papers were now all sorted. She leafed to a blank page in her ring-bound notepad, pulled her calculator close and started pulling numbers together. A few hours later, she rubbed the back of her neck, got up and made herself tea and drank it in the armchair next to the sofa. She sat before the crackle and fine aroma of the Sweetwood in the fireplace, mixed with the soothing heart-bush tea that steamed gently into her face. She looked up at the mantle at the picture of Eli, Mahlon and Kleon holding the repainted sign in front of the store. The boys had paint marks all over their faces, hands and clothes. Eli was grinning, likely because Naomi was behind the camera scolding him about how hard it would be to get oil paint out of the boys' clothes.

"The winery folks," Naomi said, thinking aloud after draining her teacup. The owners of the wineries were among the few who could afford and possibly make use of an empty shop in the heart of the town.

"And Bo."

She smirked as she looked at the wall clock. Ruth still wasn't home.

"If Bo is interested, it could be him. I'd feel better if it were him," she whispered. Making her way back to the home office, she started whistling one of the songs Ruth had been practicing for Sabbath service. The new songs they were coming up with were quite sweet. Naomi relished knowing them before they were introduced in service. Singing along as soon as the choir started singing made it easier for her to keep her eyes closed while she sang. Not seeing Eli with the ushers still made her chest hurt. Thirty years of saving his seat until he came to join her had left her putting her purse and bible on the seat beside her every week. Having someone tap her on the shoulder to ask if the seat was taken and having to say no each time had pushed her to stop carrying a purse and bible.

"That screen behind the stage is too bright though," she murmured as she opened the door and inhaled the combination of furniture polish and air freshener.

***

A few weeks later, Ruth and Naomi were lounging in the backyard, facing Naomi's iridescent garden, replete with a collage of vibrant hues. Butterflies, bumblebees and ladybugs danced through the canopy of flowers. Naomi sighed, frowned and peered over at Ruth who was giggling at something on her phone. She had put off asking Bo about buying the store for months to avoid creating any kind of awkwardness for Ruth. But the other store owners had all moved their things out and it bothered her that Eli's store was sitting unused.

"Ruru?"

"Yes, Mamma Nay?" Ruth put her phone down on the coffee table between them and turned to fully face Naomi.

"I want to ask Bo to buy El's business license and property," Naomi said. Ruth's eyes widened, then she frowned and rubbed her face.

"Uh, I can ask him if you want. I'm texting him right now. I didn't know there was a problem with selling it. Do we need money? I can take up some night shifts at the winery,"

Ruth said, reaching for her phone. Naomi smiled and raised her hand.

"No dear. There's no money issue. I simply want the business to stay in the family. Eli worked hard to build it up. It'd be a shame to sell it to someone we don't know. The bank has been calling me to say that a few foreigners want to buy it. That's all," Naomi said. Ruth sighed and lowered her hand slightly, letting the phone dangle.

"Oh, thank God. I was wondering how come you hadn't told me we needed money. Okay, so how come you didn't ask Bo before now?"

"I didn't want to interrupt your courtship," Naomi said. Ruth beamed.

"Mamma Nay, that's really sweet of you but Bo is a businessman. He can compartmentalise," Ruth said, she started blushing and giggling and Naomi barked a quick laugh before catching herself.

"You two are adorable." Naomi said, picking up her teacup. "Don't text him about that. I'll go and see him tomorrow."

"Great! I'm sure he'll be happy to see you," Ruth said, still blushing.

"Good. Now, when are you two getting married, I'd like grandchildren please and thank you," Naomi said, grinning behind the cup of tea. Ruth blushed and laughed until her face was red.

"I'm not the one proposing so don't ask me," she said, winking. Naomi smirked and mouthed "Okay."

"Wait, don't ask Bo either!" Ruth said, sitting upright and shaking her head vigorously.

***

Naomi smiled and nodded to herself as she got off the electric scooter Bo had gifted her and parked it beside the house. Going to therapy for the last two years hadn't been anywhere near as bad as she'd thought it would be. She went around to the back, humming. She wanted to pull the few weeds she'd glimpsed before going to town to meet her therapist. The first six months had been an almost constant heartache but by the time she stopped to think about it, more than a year had passed since the last time she'd felt the pang of pain when someone talked about Eli or her sons. It helped that the therapist was an outsider who visited town, did sessions and then left and went home to the city. As she bent down and got to work, she began humming one of the songs they'd sung last sabbath.

Twenty-three minutes into her work, Naomi rose from her knees, pulled off her gardening gloves and fished out her phone from her pocket. Ruth was calling. Naomi frowned, then shrugged. Ruth and Bo were supposed to visit later for dinner. Unless she was calling to cancel.

She almost never misses Wednesday dinner though. And Bo loves my cooking.

"Hello dear, is everything okay?" she asked.

"Mamma Nay!" Ruth said, her voice was almost a shriek. Naomi adjusted the volume on her end.

"Hi Ruru, what's going on dear?"

"I'm pregnant! You're gonna be a grandma!"

Gamara

(Gomer)

Gamara Dibla swept strawberry blonde hair with cherry red-highlights over one shoulder, smiled, blew a kiss and clicked the red circle on her screen. Sitting up from the contorted position she'd been lying in, she reached for her clothes and pulled on her blouse. Her neck was stiff, and her face hurt from all the talking she'd done in that session. She slid from the four-poster king bed that was too big for the bedroom. The silky sheets she'd been wrapped in slipped from the bed, twisted around her ankles. After releasing herself, she went into the living area where her chest of drawers and other furniture were. The fan who had bought her the bed was adamant on getting her a king-sized bed. It was stupid, but they liked seeing her in it.

In her bathroom, she scrubbed her face to remove the makeup to reveal the light brown freckles that formed a constellation in her face. Her phone vibrated causing her to shiver. The alarm notification let her know that church was in twenty-five minutes. She showered again, mostly for the feeling of the hot water on her neck and back.

The familiar roiling in the pit of her stomach and the heat in her chest cascaded through her as she thought about what people at the church would think if they knew where her tithe came from. She liked the music and the people at the church were mostly nice. There were no complaints about the amounts she put into the offering plate. But they'd look at her sideways if they knew she made money showing her body to thirsty men online.

As she pulled on a pair of blue jeans and a loose crew neck cherry red blouse, she could hear whoever lived upstairs stomping across their apartment and slamming doors behind them.

"See, this is why I don't have a roommate," she said, shaking her head. There were arguments between roommates in half the apartments in her building. They argued in the halls, she heard them through the walls, they bickered in the laundry room.

Hopping onto her strawberry red electric bike, she set out for the church that was only six minutes away from her apartment. Around her, the city buildings stretched like yawning giants into the air. The bike traffic lanes were almost as full as the rush hour vehicular traffic trying to work its way from one end of the city to the other. Gamara rode past her favourite coffee shop, allowing the bike and the slight decline in the road to do most of the work. As usual, there were couples smooching and taking selfies and feeding each other dessert. She rolled her eyes and weaved around an old lady who was just getting onto a scooter.

Half these guys watch girls like me all the time. She thought. Most of the regulars who watched had rings on when they tuned in for video calls. The others who didn't wear a ring, wanted to say things to her that they couldn't say to their own partners.

"Maybe they'd make me stop attending," she said to herself as she rounded the final corner unto the street where the church building sat. Shrugging, she let the bike cruise down the sidewalk. She'd had the thought many times in the last year since she'd been attending but the truth was that she had no intention of giving up her income. School had made her a ball of nerves, working in fast food and grocery stores had put her on anxiety meds for over a year.

She took up her regular seat at the back, in the middle of the row. The associate pastor looked her way, again, and waved. She nodded curtly and turned to face the pulpit. He'd been doing that since she first started attending, even when she came late and slipped in among the crowds. His striking eyes and soft smile were unnerving.

Does he know me from the sites? Gamara wondered, she'd seen church guys on her page before, shaming her in the comment section after she'd ignored their direct messages. He was handsome and seemed like a decent guy though. Unless he used an alias, she hadn't seen anyone like him. He probably would have called her out by now to get props from the rest of the church. He taught the Bible studies on Wednesdays and taught a class for those new to the faith. A few times when she'd been grocery shopping or getting her hair done, she'd seen him feeding some of the folks who lived on the street as well.

Shaking her head, she closed her eyes and embraced the lovely music rolling from the stage through the pews.

He's just being nice. Or he knows about me and is 'praying for me to change'.

***

Nausea threatened her all day. She gagged and retched as she posted videos and texting fans and packing the items for shipping that they'd paid for. Admin days were usually her favourite. No makeup, no camera, just her blanket pajamas. This time, her mom had called. Gamara dry heaved and pushed the laptop away, stalking into the kitchenette for her water bottle. The conversation was still playing in her head.

"Amy's graduation is next month, are you coming?"

"I can try mom."

"Oh, that would be lovely dear. Amy says William is coming. I bet he'd wanna see you." Her mom had sounded so cheery mentioning that stain of a man. Gamara had gritted her teeth through the rest of the call. As her mom spoke about her sister's dress and who the valedictorian was, Gamara was bombarded with memories of slimy smiles, drunken breath and welts on her back and legs that had left scars and were the reason she owned commercial sized tubs of concealer.

Of course, William wants to see me, he wants to see me flinch when he hugs me. He wants to take pictures to show his friends his daughter and stepdaughter who he 'raised' into lovely young women.

"Mom?"

"Yes, dear?"

Her mom had been saying something about the whole family wearing maroon to match Amy's school colours or something of the sort. Gamara had caught herself before asking her question. Asking her mom why she obviously still cared about William–even though he'd left for a younger woman years ago–would likely have ended in her mom losing it on the phone. Gamara shuddered. It wouldn't have been fair to Amy for Gamara to set her mom off and cause her to not talk to anyone for six months again.

"I have clients waiting, so I have to go. I'll let you know if I can come to the graduation."

That call had ended before ten that morning. Gamara was still reeling from it. Scrolling on her phone had not stopped her from remembering William call her sweetheart while he slapped her across the face or took his belt to her legs while he was drunk. Eating mango sorbet straight from the container did not chill the dread in her stomach at the thought of him smiling before beating her for not getting straight A's on her report card.

"This is for your own good, sweetheart. Next time you'll remember to work harder." That had been his favourite line. Gamara ran to the bathroom and threw up. Sliding to the floor beside the toilet, she murmured.

"Mom, you sure know how to pick them huh?"

***

The associate pastor had been clenching and unclenching his fists in the hallway between the staff offices and the main church hall when Gamara walked in for the early service the next Sunday. He waved stiffly with a clearly forced smile. She nodded and beelined for her usual seat. It was like passing the principal in the hallway in high school.

Did he find out about me? she thought. Moments later, he walked out of the hall and into the main building and headed straight for the back row in the pews. Smiling at the few early congregants, he rolled up his sleeves to above his elbows as he walked. The first service on Sundays usually saw lower attendance than the second service, making it easy to pass the few people sitting in her row.

Why is he in my row? He has his own seat up front. Not like this, please.

He sidestepped his way into the row and sat right next to her. Her heartbeat became as loud as the drums playing on the stage. Refusing to look at him, she kept lifting her hands and singing along with the worship team.

"Pardon me," he said as the lead pastor transitioned from worship to the announcements. "I'd like to talk with you after church if that's alright."

Not like this. Gamara thought to herself. *He does know, I'm getting put out of the church. Well at least he's not announcing it from up there.*

She shuddered at the thought of her name being called from the pulpit. She barely ever showed her face in her recordings and pictures, but fans sometimes paid extra for face to face. As she sat down for the announcements, her mind reeled, scanning every fan name she could remember and considering everything she posted that possibly had her face in it.

How did he find out?

What's a pastor doing on those sites?

Where will I find another church that's close to home?

For the rest of the service, her heart did a drum solo in her chest. She barely heard the message and wrote no notes on her phone for the first time in many months.

My last service and I can't even enjoy it. Stupid jerk. Could've just come and gotten me now instead of at the beginning of service. She remained standing after the closing prayer, expecting him to walk her out. He sat. Tilting her head to look down at him, she shrugged and sat also.

"Thank you," he said gently, his voice low. "I'll keep this as succinct as possible. The Lord spoke to me about you in a dream. Two people I trust confirmed my dream with things they'd heard from the Lord as well. Basically, I believe the Lord wants me to marry you." Gamara stopped grimacing long enough to process the words that were hitting her unprepared ears. Turning, she went from scrunched brows to outright gaping at him. He had a tattoo peeking out from where he'd rolled up the sleeves of a cyan dress shirt.

"Uh, what now? Are you messing with me?" her thoughts crumbled. There's no way she'd heard him right.

Why would God... About her... What?

"Why?" she managed, wrestling with her unravelling composure. Hosea shrugged and she immediately felt the urge to punch him. Smiling, he raised both hands, palms facing her.

"It will take a while to explain. Not sure if you know about how God sometimes just tells people stuff. But it's a real thing. I'm not toying with you." He said, his smile was not helping.

"I know God does whatever He pleases," Gamara snapped in a whisper, glancing around at the dwindling number of congregants, some of whom were looking their way. She cringed.

"I mean, why would he tell a pastor to marry me?" she said out of the corners of her mouth while trying to wrench her face back to neutrality. "He knows what I do for a living, but do you?"

Hosea's smile faltered briefly then flickered back to full.

"I do. I believe the Lord has seen your heart towards Him. And to be completely honest, I saw you and was drawn to you before He confirmed the word," he said. Gamara made a face and rolled her eyes at him. Big surprise, it was because she was attractive.

"Listen, I'm not sure y'all prayed hard enough," she said, straightening and snatching up her purse. "I'm a model, men find me attractive. I don't think attraction is a sin, but lust is. You're a pastor, I'm what I am. Just acknowledge that you think I'm hot, repent for whatever you've thought up and go find a proper church girl to marry. Don't do this."

Her purse and phone in hand, she stood and turned to leave the aisle. Hosea grimaced, then chuckled.

"And isn't there a scripture about a virtuous woman? I don't qualify."

"You're fiery. And you know some Scripture. Colour me impressed," he said, standing. He was taller than her–as tall as William. His presence behind her made her cringe. She hadn't been this close to a male in a while. She did not miss it.

"Colour me annoyed. Also, the next girl you do this to, do it in your office and not in the open like this," Gamara shot back and walked away.

"I apologize for annoying you. Please pray about it. I'll see you at Bible study or at first service next week. I believe the Lord will speak to you as well," he said, after catching up to her back. Gamara fanned him off and kept walking, exiting the building as fast as her legs would go. He did not pursue.

She rode home as usual, slipping around slower riders and making it home in nine minutes. Now she was all set up for her usual routine. She had recordings to do. But every time she turned on the camera, her hand hovered over the record button. For twenty minutes, she sat staring at the screen until it timed out and she had to awaken it. After the fifth time tapping the screen, she rolled her eyes and searched for Hosea

Beyari. His socials reminded her of the guys who sometimes stalked her, Stock photos and AI renderings of bible stuff were all he posted. The last time he'd posted a selfie was when he was in high school. The only good pictures of him were from the church social media page. Gamara huffed and closed the page. After slapping her face with her palms, she took a deep breath, checked the view count on her last post and launched the camera.

"He'll have me out of his system by next week. Everyone always said, 'God told me', pssh. Lying on God to land a partner is crazy," Gamara said. She tapped the record button and got to work. Her last post was already trending down.

The following Wednesday, Gamara stormed into the church an hour early and banged on Hosea's office door. A few seconds later, the door opened to reveal a smiling Hosea, hazel eyes seemingly producing their own light.

"Hello, Gamara."

She flushed and stepped back, his smile making her want to punch his straight nose.

"You planted a stupid idea in my head and now I'm dreaming about you. What the heck dude?" she said. Hosea continued smiling and beckoned her into the office. She glared at him.

"What did you dream?"

"I dreamt about you, stupid," she snapped. He was still smiling. He had nice teeth.

"Anything else?"

His tone was so even that Gamara was tempted to flip him off and storm out of the building. She hesitated with her mouth open. Hosea leaned against the door post and folded his arms. Rolling her eyes, Hagar swallowed words she had no intention of using inside a church.

"Your dad was a soldier?"

"Yes, he was." Hosea answered, his smile became a grin.

"I don't even know how I know that; I just woke up knowing. How does that even happen? It's creepy," Gamara said. Shooing him into the office, she followed and closed the door. The church had been empty when she walked through to get to his office, he was always there it seemed.

"It's not that creepy. But yeah, my dad was in the navy and there's no way you'd have known that unless you broke into a government server or something," he said. Gamara rolled her eyes at him.

I asked the Holy Spirit to show you something you wouldn't know on your own to prove it to you," he said. He sat in his chair as soon as she'd taken a seat in one of the chairs before his desk. The desktop was sparse. Other than his laptop and bible, there was only a large notepad with barely legible handwriting and a cellphone. The office itself was barely decorated. The only touch of personality was a degree certificate on the wall to her left and a lone Ficus in the corner behind Hosea. It dawned on her that the room was silent, so she turned to him and rolled her eyes.

"I make videos online."

"I know."

"Men have seen my body."

"I know."

"I make money that way, it's my job."

"Yup," Hosea said. Gamara couldn't read his face. She scowled and crossed her arms.

"What exactly is happening here? Is this God's way of telling me to go get a 'real' job?"

"You'll have to ask Him that, I only know what He told me."

"Which is what? 'Marry the internet model' and then what?" Gamara said, lacing her words with as much ice as possible. Hosea shrugged, smiling.

The dream about his father hadn't been the first or only dream since she'd seen Hosea the week before. She'd also dreamt about kissing him, twice. He'd weaseled his way into her psyche with his semi-formal dress shirts and stupid smile. Was it because he was a pastor? Was it because he represented something better than the idiots she'd known? It didn't matter; he'd want to change her and make her into some kind of church lady. She just liked the services. She wasn't even baptised.

"I don't trust you. And I have no way to prove this is God. The thing about your dad could be a coincidence, or you could be lying. I think you're lying. But I'm not the one preaching on a stage. I'll probably get hit with lightning for something, but it won't be that," she said. Hosea laughed and leaned back in his chair. His laugh sounded like a spring breeze caressing her face.

"God isn't Zeus. That's not how that works," he said once he finished laughing.

"I won't take your word for it."

Gamara shook her head, stood and turned to leave.

"Say I did believe you, what happens now?" she said over her shoulder.

"Gamara Dibla, would you allow me to take you to dinner this Saturday?" he asked, rising from his seat.

"Ugh," Gamara said, rubbing her face and then running her fingers through her hair. She hadn't been on a real date in years. She didn't own a dress.

"Fine."

God, if this is you, it isn't funny. You could've just told me to quit or kicked me out of your church.

<u>Nine months later</u>

Hosea had made it home after dropping her off at her apartment. She changed into a cozy pair of pink bunny footie pajamas, went to her desk and checked her fan accounts. She hadn't recorded a new video in months. For a while, she'd reposted old videos to great success. She also hadn't done a live video chat since her first date with Hosea.

"I can do this," she whispered repeatedly while clicking between the tabs of her fan pages and her bank account. She stopped on her main fan page. The one that paid her rent. Her finger hovered over the 'delete account' button. For months, she'd been psyching herself up to deactivating the accounts. She had a nice sum saved. And the degree William and her mom had forced her to finish. There had to be jobs that would hire her at entry level at least. Accounting standards surely hadn't changed much in five years.

She clicked back over to her bank account summary. The three transactions after her most recent deposit were her tithe, a transfer to her savings account, and a donation to the food bank at the women's shelter. She palmed her face and ran her hands through her hair.

"Dammit."

Sighing, she closed the laptop, put it on the empty side of the bed and curled up around her body pillow.

She squeezed her eyes shut, then opened them to stare at nothing in particular until another wave of giddiness hit her and she shuddered. He'd kissed her on the forehead again. She blushed as she remembered the first time he'd done it three months ago. They hadn't shared a kiss on the lips, yet. Gamara shook her head in disbelief and rolled over in bed until she was staring out the window at the voluminous clouds that filled the skyline. He'd been adamant that they shouldn't kiss or anything else.

"It'll cloud our judgement," was what he'd said. Gamara had shrugged. Being single for almost a decade had made it easy to go at whatever pace he set.

"Besides, if I kiss him, he'll want more and then I'll just be another body to him," she said as she reached for her phone. His social media page was still open in a tab from the last time she'd gone there. There were already pictures of the two of them from the date they'd just had. She scrolled past picture after picture of them at the park, making meals for the homeless, driving go-karts, bowling. Every time they went for a date, he handed her his phone for her to capture the moment. Then, as soon as she went to the ladies' room, she'd get pinged on her phone about being tagged in a new post.

She scrolled until she reached the picture of that third Saturday evening when he'd taken her to dinner at a restaurant she'd never heard of. No surprise, it was owned by one of the members of the church. The pics of the food that she had posted on her own page made her mouth water every time she saw them. They'd carefully prepared a meal she'd only ever seen on the internet. The smell of amazing food on tables all around them and the tasteful ambient lighting weren't the reasons she was currently staring at the pictures with shimmering eyes.

The first thing he'd asked after they finished their meal was if she was opposed to telling him about herself. The way he'd kept his phone in his pocket and looked right at her had caused her to flinch. When guys saw her through a screen, they saw a collection of body parts with a nice hairdo and makeup. Hosea met her gaze and held it. When she'd gone against her instincts and told him thing she hadn't told anyone in years, he'd taken in the whole thing without interrupting or showing any disgust.

As they drove across the city to her apartment that night, he followed up by telling her about his own life. He'd grown up in church and in a healthy nuclear family.

"My dad is lactose intolerant, so he never left to get milk."

When he'd made the joke, and was grinning to himself, Gamara had rolled her eyes and stared at him, deadpan. The lack of trauma in his life was staggering, intimidating even. The man she'd been forced to call dad had never physically left to get milk, but he might as well have. Gamara had rarely seen him wear an honest smile, and never at her. She grimaced.

"What am I doing? Momma ended up stuck with that man for the sake of kids she never wanted," she murmured and locked her phone screen and threw the phone down on the bed. Her mind was going there again. She let it. She always did.

"I'm too damaged to get married. And no man stays this sweet forever, after the honeymoon, the honey runs out," she said. She reached for her phone again and pulled up his name in her contact list. Her finger hovered over the block button. There was another church on the other side of town that wasn't terribly far by e-bike. And Hosea's church streamed services online if she wanted to hear the choir. He'd go look at her pictures, satisfy whatever delusion was pulling him and then choose one of the church girls who kept looking at her funny when he walked over to talk to her after service on Sundays.

She couldn't press the button. Photos formed against her closed eyelids like film in dark rooms. Her forehead tingled from where he'd let his lips linger. She was sure she could smell the aloe and cucumber lip balm that he'd gently stolen from her a month before.

"No. No. No," she said as she got up from bed, and paced the room.

"I'm gonna end up like mom."

Two days later, Gamara sat curled up on the thrifted cerulean bean bag in the corner of her living room, next to the chest of drawers. She was awash with cold sweats. Rivulets of mascara laden tears streaked down her cheeks. Her lipstick was smeared on the right side of her cheeks and the alcohol pad she'd used to drag it from her lips. Strawberry blonde hair clung to her face. Hosea's name ran across the top of the phone screen. The call timer was still going as the phone sat on the floor, screen cracked from when she'd flung it from her ear.

He'd called her sweetheart three times, before it sunk into her subconscious and erupted burning memories and clouds of anguish. His voice wasn't William's, but she heard the belt, every time he said it. When she'd said, "I'm not anyone's sweetheart," he'd said, "It's just a term of endearment, because I care about you." William had cared too, enough to keep a belt with her name on it. Enough to hit her where it wouldn't show in public. Enough to call her a stupid little sweetheart who had nothing going for her but looks.

The call ended and Hosea tried calling back. She kicked the phone away. The old welts on her thighs caught her eye and she started trembling until she was shaking and thumping her back against the wall behind the bean bag. She shook until her shoulders ached and her back crumpled, causing her to slump sideways with her head on the floor.

She woke to the alarm for her morning run.

Not the worst way to escape nightmares. She thought, heaving herself off the floor and sauntering to her bedroom. It was 5am. According to the forecast, it was nice and cool outside, perfect for a jog. She flung herself into the thick comforters and body pillow atop her bed.

"No run today."

She posted no videos for the next three days. Her inboxes were full of fans 'checking on her'.

Her call log and text message app were both full of messages from Hosea. Walking past the half boxes of delivery meals that she didn't remember ordering or eating, she dragged herself to the bathroom and plopped down on the toilet. The glimpse of her hair she'd caught in the mirror said, "comb me, please." She snorted a chuckle at the idea of her hair talking to her and rubbed her face until she was awake enough to flush, wash her hands and stumble her way back to bed.

"I need more sorbet and wine. Can I order that?"

***

The doorbell signalled the arrival of either her dinner or whatever she'd ordered while half asleep after eating a large tub of peach ice cream.

"Leave it at the door, thanks," she called, her blouse stopped at her navel and she wasn't about to put on pants.

"Gamara, it's me. Can we talk please?" Hosea's voice hit her like a splash of cold water to the face.

Nope. We're not doing this. At all. She thought as she ran back to her room and stuffed her earbuds into her ears.

He'll get embarrassed and leave. Yeah.

A few hours later, her stomach rumbled like vibrating phones. Reaching for her tablet, she checked to see that her food had indeed been left at the door. She hopped out of bed and weaved her way across the littered floor. Humming the tune, she'd fallen asleep to, she opened the door just enough to snag the food, stooped and reached out, only to see a shoe.

"Hi Gamara," Hosea said, his voice too soft, "can we please talk?"

Why in God's name is he still here?

She flung open the door, stood, stared up at him, her eyes dark with rage.

"Fine! You want to talk, I'll talk. Leave me alone! Go to hell or heaven or whatever!" Her chest heaved. He held her gaze.

"I don't want anything to do with you!" Hosea took one step forward. Gamara hesitated then stepped back into the apartment. Placing her food in her hand, he side-stepped her, bent down and started picking up the items strewn on the floor.

"What are you doing?" she yelled. She reached out to snatch his arm then recoiled under the weight of a flashback of getting slapped in the face when she'd tried to stop William from hitting Amy.

"Stop it, leave me alone, go home Hosea! I'm gonna call the cops," she said. Her voice was held together by trembling wrath. Hosea paused, looked up at her, smiled and reached for another discarded item.

"Go ahead, I'll turn myself in," he said. Gamara tilted her head and stared at him.

"What? Why are you here?"

He reached for the last few pieces, stood up and deposited them into her bin.

"I love you."

"That's too bad."

"I'm allowed to love who I want."

"Do whatever you want then," she said, arms flailing, "leave my apartment!"

"There's still more you wanna yell about. So, I'm staying until you're done. I'll keep cleaning until you run out of steam." He walked over to the kitchenette and whisked the broom into a sweeping motion. Gamara's vision blurred. She wobble-walked her way over to the bean bag and fell into it. Hosea continued sweeping. Gamara glared at him.

"I swear I'm gonna call the police if you don't leave."

"I believe you. They'll take long enough to get here that I can get this place back to how you normally keep it."

Gamara screamed and flung the container of food at him. It splattered against his back and spilled to the floor. When he turned and bent to clean it up, her vision swam red. Words vaulted from her mouth like a broken hydrant. Images of men in her past—William, ex-boyfriends, teachers who had tried to sleep with her for a grade, the first guy she'd sold pictures of her body to—swam in and out of her vision. She could barely see the sweeping silhouette through her tears and rage. When the words began spluttering and losing steam, she dropped her no longer animated arms onto her lap and released the tears.

A soggy outline walked over to her and knelt before her.

"I'm not sure what I said that brought all this up. But I am sorry." The blur of his face before her unlocked another deluge. She cupped her face in her hands.

"Men suck," she sobbed.

"Fair. Are you opposed to me kissing your forehead?" Gamara sniffled and looked at him through her fingers.

He's a lunatic. Or maybe I am. She thought, shaking her head.

"My stepdad used to call me sweetheart while beating me."

"Oh no. That's messed up. Noted. Never again," Hosea said.

"I haven't showered."

"Is that a yes?"

"Yes, you may kiss my forehead." His lips were warm; his beard tickled the bridge of her nose. He smelled of shea butter and coconut oil—both of which she'd bought him. He was wearing that aqua dress shirt with the sleeves cuffed at his elbows and the cologne he'd worn on their first date.

"I ordered more food for you, and groceries." His voice came from across the room. She looked up to see him standing in the doorway.

"Call me when you feel up to it. That can be a year from now, or five. I'd prefer if it wasn't five though," he said. She smiled, wiped her nose on the back of her hands and nodded.

"What if it's ten years?"

"Then we'd probably have to adopt kids when we're ready," he said, shrugging. Gamara chuckled. The rhythm of laughter flowing from her chest made her pause and breathe. Her shoulders and jaw relaxed.

"Okay, I won't wait that long then," she said. He nodded and closed the door.

-END-

The Scarlet Pulse:

- By. Dr Delzetha E Sinclair

The loom was warped by time,
But the thread?
The thread never snapped.
A scarlet line of prophecy—
A pulse, a rhythm, a jagged, living rhyme.
From the mother's stitched-on banner
To the son's modern, bleeding refrain—
We are weaving the glory back,
Scrubbing the soul until we wash out the stain.

Listen—as we tear back the pages of the Old,
To sit with these women, resurrected in our time.

Khavah: The First Sunrise
She stands where the sunrise stings the factory glass,
A thirty-six-foot monument to everything that had to pass.
She is the breath of Agro-growth, the sweat in the vats,
Where simmering fruit turns the air into a heavy, sweet sauna.
Cotton clings to her like a secret;

She is no longer a "fallen" thing.
She is the morning's sight,
Taking the fruit of knowledge and forging a world of steel—
A heart on a journey,
A spirit that finally learned how to feel.

Hagar: The Prophet of the Sands

She breathes the musty wool and the reek of sheep dung,
A housemaid in a manor where the songs are left unsung.
Dawn-to-dusk labour, a chore that never ends,
With a spine that's bowing and a knee that barely bends.
Look at her eyes—red lines scrambling 'round the brown,
Crows' feet decades early, a weary, heavy crown.
Then comes the "intimate connection":
The catheter, the syringe, the clinical lack—
Carrying a legacy for a man who won't look back.
She waddles through the basement, ankles throbbing in her shame,
Then staggers from the bath to the taxi with no name.
But the scarlet in her status is the fire in her bones—
The prophet of the parched who finds water in the stones.

Tamar: Architect of Justice

The tang of raw blood is souring her mouth,
From singing out her soul while the judges look south.
Six days of riffs and runs, of "rhythms" and "rifles,"
While her lower back throbs and her spirit nearly stifles.
She sits in the studio, bob-cut clinging to her cheek,
Watching predatory arms find the "vocalists" they seek.
She heard the menacing baritone, the feet in the hall,
The "Judah" who promised her the rise before the fall.
Now she's the rebel midwife, screaming into a stuffed toy,
Fighting legal transcripts for the truth they would destroy.
She turned the jagged shards into a sovereign, sacred whole,
Scribing her victory in the flame of a resilient soul.

Naomi: The Harvest of the Heart

She walked the road of Mara until the hollow air turned sweet.
She felt the lonely echoes of a house,
The dust of Moab on her feet.
She watched six men carry her sons to a plot of public dirt,

Scowling at the "hugs" that couldn't reach the depth
of the hurt.
She is the empty vessel the Spirit chose to refill,
A testament of loyalty standing iron-willed on the
hill.
Her story is a liturgy of return through the winter
storm,
A scarlet thread of sisterhood that keeps the frozen
spirit warm.

The Final Voices: Barbara, Gamara, Farah, & Simone
Clawing out of nightmares and sweat-soaked sheets,
Smelling the smoke of Cain's end while the young
girls find retreat.
Farah and Simone, standing against the "evil" of the
buyback,
While Gamara feels the "sweetheart" fist of a stepdad's
attack.
These are the modern echoes, the women the canon
ignored,
Walking through a modern land with a voice like a
sharpened sword.
Beautifully heretical, our sovereignty takes wing—
We are not the scandal; we are the sovereign song we
continue to sing.

The scarlet you once stitched is a banner, loud and bright,
A bridge between the generations, burning through the night.
The specialist has taught the craft; the son has drawn the line.
In this Heart Journey of the soul,
The scarlet thread is—and has always been—divine.

Acknowledgements

When I was 16, **Dr Delzetha Sinclair**, my mum, and my English teacher at the time, made our class write a poem. I'd never written a poem in my life, but I'd always loved literature (also thanks to her). That poem is the reason I went on to write hundreds of poems and pursue writing long-form fiction for almost two decades.

In 2021, I reconnected with a friend who has now become closer than a brother. **Robert Hall** took time to see me, hear me, and hold space for me as I navigated a whole lot of life. Thanks to his friendship, validation, and holding me accountable, I finally wrote and finished a novel and got feedback that propelled me into writing what has now become *Retold: Heart Journeys*.

I also want to thank **Paula-Kaye Taylor**, **Sophia Richards**, **Alicia Richards,** and **Deanielle Green** for taking the time to read my work and give me tangible and helpful feedback that helped shape how I write.

About the Author

Nikolai-Andre Alexander has spent more than two decades writing poetry, short fiction, and novels that explore the emotional and spiritual tensions of human life. A devoted student of Scripture, he approaches the Bible not only as sacred text, but as a vast narrative populated by real people—individuals wrestling with faith, doubt, love, loss, courage, and consequence.

Coming from a family of educators and lifelong readers, Nik developed an early reverence for language, literature, and learning. His writing seeks to bring ancient stories into conversation with the modern world, illuminating the humanity within the pages of Scripture and inviting readers to see its characters not as distant figures of legend, but as people navigating struggles that remain deeply familiar today.

Through his work, he hopes to draw fresh attention to the beauty, complexity, and enduring relevance of the biblical story.

He is the father of one, an avid reader, and—by his own admission—a proud Bible nerd.

www.ingramcontent.com/pod-product-compliance
Lightning Source LLC
LaVergne TN
LVHW091127080826
845145LV00008B/2067

* 9 7 8 1 0 6 9 8 8 1 4 0 3 *